MW01105320

THE SHROUD SOCIETY

'I want you to kill my wife,' Rushton said. Rushton, a tycoon faced with treachery, could see no other way to save his crumbling empire, for his wife, Rena, had absconded with a set of illegal accounts as potentially dangerous as a triggered time-bomb. Storer, a professional killer, nodded, shook hands on the deal and walked out into the biggest gamble of his life – a high-wire trip of deceit and double-cross with a woman he dared not trust, and a cool half million prize for the hardest heart in the game. If Rena refused to die, there was always her sister, Kathy, a lush young nightclub singer, to take her place as the corpse. That was the plan; a cold-blooded overture to blackmail and violent death, with conscience the only factor which nobody took into the reckoning.

THE SHROUD SOCIETY

Robert Crawford

First published 1969
by
Constable & Co Ltd
This edition 1993 by Chivers Press
published by arrangement with
the author

ISBN 0 7451 8620 3

British Library Cataloguing in Publication Data available

Printed and bound in Great Britain by
Redwood Books, Trowbridge, Wiltshire

FOREWORD

ROBERT CRAWFORD, author of this gripping novel, has his own band of devoted followers, and rightly so. Perhaps not all of them will be aware that the name is only one of the many *noms de plume* of the prolific Hugh C Rae (others are James Albany, R B Houston, Stuart Stern, Jessica Stirling).

Under his own name, he gave us the popular Inspector McCaig series, in which readers were treated to an exploration of the mores of the criminal fraternity north of the border, together with an intensive course of the local vernacular. The overall effect is to produce a 'Scottishness' which is unique in my reading experience.

What the reader looks for in a crime novel is largely a matter of individual preference, and for me a prime requisite is a convincing backcloth. If, for example, a story is taking place in a South American republic, it is not sufficient to name people Manuel or Pedro and make passing references to straw hats and donkeys. These are no more than window-dressing and, in the absence of more authenticating material, quickly spotted as such. The reader is uneasily conscious that, with a few elementary substitutions, the locale would transfer easily to France (via Marcel and onions) or Italy (Vittore and chianti). In less meticulous hands, the same could be said of a Scottish background. It takes more than a character named Angus, sprinkling his dialogue with och-ayes, to establish a convincing background.

No fear of such shortcomings with Hugh Rae's work, wherein authenticity is the keynote. He reaches outside the constricting parameters of the formula crime novel to inform us on what might be described as criminal social history, and the result is a far more satisfying read.

He also has had the good grace to recognise the sterling work of his protagonist McCaig, and ensured that this is given tangible expression by regular promotion. Eventually, we are reading about the Superintendent, which is only just. Too many authors are remiss in such matters, and are still expecting a by-now disgruntled Inspector Dogsbody to produce results after twenty or more years, without even a mention of higher rank.

Hugh C Rae has been steeped in the writing environment for all his adult life, having begun his working career with the Glasgow antiquarian booksellers John Smith and Son. He has now been a full-time writer for almost thirty years, and is currently lecturer in creative writing at the University of Glasgow. He was also a founder-member of the Association of Scottish Writers.

In the story you are about to read, the author provides a good demonstration of his adaptability. No closed community here, no gradual gathering of assorted clues in a confined locality. To begin with, the central character is a professional assassin, scarcely calculated to arouse our sympathy, but our interest is immediate. What kind of person sets himself such a course? A psychopath perhaps, or someone born without the ability to distinguish between right and wrong?

Not so. This man, Storer, is simply providing a service. Clearly someone of above-average intelligence, his façade is one of cold-blooded indifference to the suffering he inflicts on his victims and others. We are privileged to see behind this exterior and learn something of his thought-processes, as he waits in lonely hotel rooms and rainy car parks. He has a particular and new problem in *The Shroud Society*, for he has never previously contracted to kill a woman. It annoys him to find that the question of gender should cause him any qualms. It also immediately involves the reader, because this is an inescapable dilemma, and its resolution is integral to the development of the story.

To tell you anything of what follows would be to spoil your enjoyment of this fast-paced and intriguing novel, which is far from my purpose.

Please read on.

PETER CHAMBERS

Peter Chambers is a former Chairman of the CWA, and the author of over sixty crime and detective books, some featuring his own 'private eye' in an imaginary California town, and others under various *noms de plume*.

THE BLACK DAGGER CRIME SERIES

The Black Dagger Crime series is a result of a joint effort between Chivers Press and a sub-committee of the Crime Writers' Association, consisting of Marian Babson, Peter Chambers and Peter Lovesey. It is designed to select outstanding examples of every type of detective story, so that enthusiasts will have the opportunity to read once more classics that have been scarce for years, while at the same time introducing them to a new generation who have not previously had the chance to enjoy them.

Part One

1

Storer stopped on the inside of the pavement and glanced up at the door. Behind the glass panels Burchill was waiting. His stockbroker's suit merged with the shadows behind the fronds of a pot-plant. If Storer had not known to look out for him Burchill could have remained invisible until the chars dragged their mops over his hand-lasted shoes. Storer went up the steps and flattened his hand against the glass. Burchill slid out from his corner, unlocked the door and admitted Storer to the building. The men nodded to each other without warmth, moved through the foyer and down an unlighted corridor to the side elevator. The elevator dragged them smoothly up to the ninth floor of the office block. Burchill silently ushered Storer through several nameless doors, and fell in behind him as he made the long walk down an aisle of desks and shrouded computing equipment to the inner office. Storer knocked. Rushton told him to come in.

The boss was framed against the slats of the venetian blind, his skin pale with the reflection of the plastic. In one fat-pouched hand he held a cigarette, in the other an ash-tray. One buttock rested on the radiator grill and his paunch stuck out, making the waistcoat wing away from the top of his pants. Tonight, Storer thought, the boss looked his age, sixty; not all his tailors or barbers or doctors could disguise it. When he spoke his voice had a trace of the old gravel in it.

The office was as big as a basketball court. Heavy brown drapes clung to the sides of the window, a curved desk had a red-leather chair like a throne behind it. A stippling of light from the desk lamp lay on the crushed cushion. Rushton came away from the window, transferred the tray and offered his free hand to Storer. Storer shook it. Though the corners of the office were dark, Storer was sure they were alone, with none of Rushton's trained apes watching every move from the shadows. Storer said nothing, waiting, loose. He was not afraid of Rushton.

Rushton sighed, and tapped ash again. He seemed embarrassed. He cleared his throat; his jowls shuddered and the rolls of fat under his eyes quivered.

'Roy,' he said.

Obediently Burchill left the room. Storer had never been alone with Rushton before. Burchill, or before Burchill, McKenna, had always been around – trusted. For an instant it crossed Storer's mind that maybe this time Burchill himself had the cross on his chest, then Rushton said, 'I want you to kill my wife.'

He dabbed the butt in the tray in his palm, not looking at Storer. The natural word on Storer's tongue was 'Why?' but he held it back. In his trade it was better not to ask questions like that and he had to be natural tonight. He had another question ready, but Rushton beat him with the answer. 'I'll give you three thousand for the right kind of job.'

'What kind of job?' Storer asked.

'To look like an accident.'

'When?'

'Soon.'

'Does she know that you want her dead?' Storer asked.

'Perhaps.'

'All right,' Storer said. 'Where is she?'

'That,' Rushton said softly, 'is part of the problem.'

'Now, wait,' said Storer. 'You mean I've got to find her first. I thought you said . . .'

'She may suppose I want her dead but that's not why she's hiding.'

Storer watched Rushton open the drawer under the desk, take out a folder and push it over to him. He lifted it and opened the flap. Inside were a list of addresses, half a dozen photographs and a stubby manilla envelope sealed with tape. Storer picked at the tape, opened the envelope and looked at the end of the money.

'Five hundred now,' said Rushton. 'The rest later. One other point, I want the black briefcase she'll have with her. That's most important.'

'All for three thousand,' Storer said. 'Bargain week.'

'We'll see,' Rushton said. 'Bring me the briefcase and we'll see.'

Storer nodded. He put the envelope in his overcoat pocket and tucked the folder into the breast so that the edge was held by his belt. He pulled his collar up. To complete the contract he shook hands with Rushton, then went out. Burchill picked him up and escorted him back to the street.

'Good night,' Burchill said.

Storer did not answer.

2

It was raining in Holborn. It was raining all over London; the same rain, thin and fine, drifting down straight without any wind. It sank softly into the nap of Storer's overcoat and soaked his hair, plastering it flat to his skull. Water ran down his face on to his collar. He did not hurry, walking with a long-legged loping gait down Chancery Lane to the spot opposite the Courts of Justice where he had parked the Porsche. He got in, started the engine and the wipers and dried his face with the towel in the glove compartment. He lit a cigarette, then took the car forward into the Strand. He weaved it cleanly through the theatre traffic which clotted round the West End, worked through Charing Cross and drove down Whitehall, sitting very light on the gas. At Victoria he pulled off into the grid of Pimlico and kept turning corners for a while until he was satisfied that he had nobody in tow. Rushton had no reason in the world to tie a can on him but Storer's caution was notorious. Eventually he threaded back into Knightsbridge and joined the river of fast traffic which flowed up past the Hilton. He gave his lingering doubts one last fling, took the Edgware Road and Marylebone, to come in to Wilcox Square from the north. He parked the Porsche where no one would bother it until Monday and hiked the quarter of a mile to the Gresham through the rain.

The Gresham was a small quiet hotel, a dozen rooms piled on top of one another. Storer had been there for four days now and liked it. The dining-room and offices were in the basement, each bedroom lay immured behind a double door off a main staircase. There was no room service to speak of, and the rooms were shabby, but Storer could come and go as he pleased with the front door key. Except in the morning when *au pairs* did the cleaning and migrant tourists changed around, he bothered nobody and nobody bothered him. He climbed to the third floor and went first to his own room. It was quiet, large and old-fashioned, with tall windows facing out into a well. He closed the curtains over them and stripped off his clothing. He washed and shaved and dressed in dry pants, pulling a sweater over his head. His hair was still damp in spite of the towelling and clung snug to his head like a Rabbi's cap. After that he brought a chair from the bedside and stood it by the Victorian wardrobe and climbed up on it. He felt over the edge of the wardrobe roof, picked out a bottle and replaced it with the unopened folder and the envelope. He climbed down again, wiping his hands on his haunches.

With the bottle in one hand and a toothglass in the other he padded barefoot from the room and climbed up one flight. He let himself through the first door into the box-like corridor with the bathroom at the end and touched his knuckle to the bedroom door.

'Storer?'

'Yeah.'

She opened the door. He went into the room. She slipped the bolt behind him and took the bottle and glass from his hands. A bedside lamp and a neon strip over the wash-basin mirror gave the room its only light.

Storer watched her as she returned to the basin, rinsed out her mouth and stuck the brush back in the plastic rack. She turned.

'Well?'

'Three thousand,' Storer told her.

She pursed her lips, full and red as if they had blood on them. When she smiled her teeth were as white as peppermint.

'I have to earn it first,' Storer said.

She sighed, conical breasts riding high against the sweater. She lay down on the carpet under the light and lifted her skirt over her waist. She lay quite still, arms by her sides, legs apart, eyes closed. She did not open her eyes until Storer touched her, then she flared them wide, round and surprised and anxious.

'You enjoy this,' she said. 'You really enjoy it, Storer, don't you?'

He covered her, and moved his hand.

'Play dead, Mrs Rushton,' he said.

3

Storer had never killed a woman before. Of the ten marks he had taken out of the game, including four for Rushton, nine had been adult Caucasian males and the tenth a Negro. None of them had been innocent or ignorant of the risks involved in playing the game and he had put them all down cleanly – except the Negro. He had fouled up on the surprise pitch and found himself struggling for his life. He got the Negro finally with the lead base of an office lamp and even now had trouble forgetting how the brains burst from the side of the blue-black skull like curly red locks and how, when he let the man slump to the lino, a tattered end-of-something in the bone-hole had sprinkled him with blood. The fabric of his suit had loved the blood so much it would not relinquish the stains to any cleaners' fluid. Not wanting any reminders of that job around him, he had jettisoned it.

Already tension was coming up too strong for comfort, grinding against the cold edge of his professionalism, maybe blunting it a little. He would be glad when it was tomorrow. If the stakes had not been so high he would never have come in on the job in the first place, but he did not have the strength of will to turn down the money. Besides, the idea of hitting into the soft white belly of Rushton's organisation appealed to the seam of irony which Storer had managed to preserve. Though he killed when necessary he took no pleasure in it. He had no truck with the psychopaths who did it for kicks. Pros who turned morbid or fell in love with the power of the job did not last long. Storer was a good pro with a string of successes going back twelve years. There was no record on him for any crime and that fact, together with his guile and intelligence, took him out of the ruck. Not only could he command a top price for his services now but he could afford to pick and choose his jobs. Only the top brass knew where to find him; though the little men in the lesser rackets might study his handiwork, to them he was only a legend. Killing was no comic operation; in spite of his control sometimes the multitude of tiny scars which the trade had inflicted on the skin of his soul smarted and stung in the sweats of the night. And he had never killed a woman.

Against his flank he felt the rise and fall of her belly and her arm lay leaden across his chest. He knew she was asleep and did not look at her. Instead he stared up at the sliver of light which split the curtain and printed itself on the high ceiling. Rushton's woman: more than that even, Rushton's wife. Until a couple of weeks ago he could not have cared less about Rushton's operations: they were none of his business. All Storer knew then was that Rushton was a big man with wealth and power, with the façade of a dozen legitimate companies to hide behind whenever strong light fell on any of his less legal transactions. Rushton could straddle the lines of the law with the agility of a sword-dancer but in recent years he had shown little flashes of carelessness which made Storer worry for him. On the front side he was a property owner with holdings in several European countries, the East and even in the USA. The manipulation of finance on an international scale gave him ample cover for gold-hoarding, smuggling and the fencing of hot money. He owned more gambling clubs than Storer had knuckles. Rushton had been practically impregnable, until he got the urge to show his respectability to the world and married Rena Arden. Storer flattered himself that he would have spotted Rena's stamp half a mile away, seen through the lush body and sophisticated veneer right to the rotten, hard-edged core of her. But he wasn't sixty and had no urge to settle down. Rushton should have known better than to trust a woman as loving as Rena, a woman thirty-odd years younger than he was. What did he expect for his money – love?

After a while Storer slid out from under her arm, dressed and moved soundlessly to the door. As his hand sought the bolt he heard her say, 'Good luck, Storer.'

'I'll see you tomorrow night,' he said. 'You know the arrangement.'

'Tonight, you mean. It's Sunday now.'

'Yes.'

'Storer?'

'What?'

'You will go through with it?'

'I always do,' he said. He found the bolt and slipped it back and turned the handle.

'I don't want her to suffer, you understand.'

'Sure,' Storer said. 'She's your sister.'

'I don't want you to . . .'

Storer closed the door on her and went back to his own room.

He washed again, set the travelling clock to wake him at six, then took the wallet from his jacket and fished out the clipping and the photograph. Sitting naked on the edge of the bed he held them under the lamp. She was younger, fresher-looking than Rena but close enough to pass. He thought again about what he must do.

It was very quiet in the room. The babble of rain cascading from a broken rhone sounded in the distance. An ambulance, or patrol car, wailed far off in the remote reaches of the city. Storer flipped the lid of his lighter and held the gas flame to the corner of the photograph, letting it eat up the pretty face. He dropped the burning card into the ash-tray and added the clipping, tamping it down with his finger until the smoke had all gone and the paper disintegrated into a few flakes of black snow.

He got into the cool clean bed and switched out the lamp. He put his hands behind his neck and breathed deeply, thinking again of all the places where Rena might have stowed the briefcase. How could he persuade her to tell him where it was when she trusted him no more than he trusted her. He did not like the woman. But the juice she brewed, alone and bored in the bedroom all day long, was too sweet to waste. She needed him just as he needed her. There was always a woman before a job.

Storer lay for a long time listening to the slow steady thump of his heart, letting details of the coming tickle percolate gently in his brain. By this hour tomorrow it would have begun, and he would be well on the way to collecting his share of a cool half-million. Thinking about the rake-off he finally fell asleep.

4

A grey Sunday rain sifted down over Manchester, reminding Storer of hoary old jokes about the city's weather. He booked into the Grosvenor Hotel and went directly to his room to shower off the grime of the train journey. After lunch he lay on the bed, fully clothed, and slept. He had no business until evening. When he wakened dusk was down like a pall over the iron surface of the river, and the traffic below his window squeaked and hissed on the wet road surface. Rain still fell, thin and granular, from a ceiling of porous cloud.

He spread out a map of the city on the bed and devised his route, muttering street names to himself so that he would have no need to ask anyone for directions. The diagrammatic patterns of houses, factories, canals, railways seemed to reduce the city to a simple cipher, without form or substance. If only he could keep it that way. Shortly after seven he stowed the map in his bag and drew out a soiled raincoat. He folded it over his arm, but the gun in the pocket was heavy and he fastened the belt around it to make a loose bag which he could hold comfortably against his chest and still reach quickly. From the overnight bag he also took a silencer. He slipped it into a long pocket specially stitched into his jacket. The short-bladed knife he tucked into another pocket, leather-trimmed, under the tails. Unless he was dealing with experts it would never be noticed: tonight he was not dealing with experts. He had a rough cloth cap with a stiff ugly brim. He stuck it on his head and grimaced at himself in the mirror; a square-featured face and a mouth without softness, just a slight quizzical lift at the corners. Ten years back, when he was in his twenties, some women might have called it a sensitive face, but not now. He tugged the cap this way and that but could not get himself to look like a railwayman or a mill-worker. He rumpled his hair and tried again, but it was no good. He stuffed the cap in his pocket and left the hotel. Outside he paused in a shop doorway and put on the coat, then set off down the rain-greased streets for the bus terminal.

The tension banded his stomach like a whalebone girdle. He thought of stopping off for a vodka but settled instead for a cup of black coffee in a Cona bar near the bus station. The coffee left a sour and bitter taste in his mouth and did nothing to relieve the ache under his ribs. The ache was familiar, part of the price he paid for being what he was. It would not affect his performance. On the upper deck of the Gorton bus he lifted his fingers from his knee and held them discreetly in front of him: rock steady. The bus filled up, the air thick with stale smoke and the smell of cheap perfume. Storer had no affinity with these people, felt nothing, not even dislike. He sat alone and isolated as the bus wended through unfamiliar streets to Winfield. The tension hardened in him until he was ready, almost eager, to get on with the job.

The Winfield Social Club was easy to find. It stood in an allotment of gravel behind a stake-fence in a side street off the main highway: a long low building of brick and wood and wired glass, already dated by its prefabricated structure. There were cars in the park around it, and a couple of empty charabancs. Groups and couples, chattering happily, moved up towards the door. In the entrance hall Storer could see the managers, bouncers and officials smiling as they inspected membership cards. He casually walked past the club to the dead end of the street. It was quiet there; the moist air formed bulbous auras around the gas lamps, the windows of the semi-detached council houses were pasted against the night sky like faded postage stamps on blotting paper. A lane led off left sneaking between an embankment and the hedge of the last house. Storer went down it, walking slowly, hands in his pockets. The banking steepened and the iron fence gave way to a wall of massive sleepers buckled against the sliding pressure of the earth above. A goods train, followed by an entourage of empty wagons, trundled overhead. Storer stood in against the hedge until it had gone, then moved on into the field behind the houses. The posts of a soccer pitch reared pale against sodden black turf scarred by players' studs from that afternoon's match. Storer followed a path along the back of the pitch to a green-painted pavilion; beyond it was the back of the club.

As he came near to the club he was greeted by a burst of applause as if his appearance roused a spontaneous welcome. The applause died into silence and then went up again, sharpened by shrill whistles and the rhythmic stamping of feet. Storer leaned on the fence. He could hear the voice of a male singer, backed by drum, piano and guitar, licking into an up-tempo number. A clink and clash of glasses over-rode the vocalist. The open door led into a kitchen or bar. He shifted on down the line of the fence until he could see into the hatch of light. Shirt-sleeved men and a dumpy woman in stained blue cotton coveralls hustled back and forth. Glassware glittered like Aladdin's cave. Crates of empty ale bottles flanked the doorway. Half hidden behind them was another doorway with a lighted pebble-glass window on either side of it. Storer hopped over the fence, crossed to this door and tried the handle. It opened and he went inside.

He found himself in a short corridor with a closed door at each end and two closed doors facing him on the inner wall. Against the blond woodwork between the doors hung two framed yellowing photographs of early steam locomotives, out of place in the modern setting. Storer turned left, opened a door and peered into another corridor. Facing him was a dressing room: a mirror with a strong light above it threw back his reflection. In the mirror too he glimpsed a girl deeper in the room. He went on into the corridor. Off to his left, the sound barely muffled by the curtain which covered the entrance, was the stage and its vocal group, three voices raised in a frantic harmony. He glanced at his watch: he was twenty minutes too early. Rena would not have arrived yet with the rented Cortina. Further up the passage was yet another door, obviously a communal dressing room for the male artistes. In it, playing cards, were two young men and an elderly gentleman who, in full make-up and evening dress, looked like a prize queen. They looked up nervously when Storer entered.

'Good evening,' Storer said, smiling. He slipped out of his raincoat and, with fingers round the gun butt, shook it and hung it on the hanger close by the door, transferring the gun discreetly to his jacket. He closed the door and came forward past the formica-topped table on which the cards lay. He heated his hands behind him at the radiator, smiling on the three men like a Cambridge tutor.

'Now,' he said, 'which are you?'

The boys glanced at each other then at the old man. The old man smiled back at Storer, a smile of understanding which waxed instantly into fawning anxiety to please. 'Agent?'

Storer held out his hand. 'Arthur Saintsbury,' he said, picking the first innocuous name which popped into his mind. 'Radleigh's.'

Flinging down his cards the old man shook Storer's hand warmly as if he was a long-lost friend. 'Radleigh's' he said. 'The *London* agency?'

'Of course,' Storer said. He wondered if there was such a firm. He released himself from the old man's grasp and nodded to the young men. They had perked up by now, but he decided to concentrate on the old man.

'You must be . . .' Storer said.

'Tommy Luton.'

'Ah,' said Storer. 'Of course. Tommy Luton. My father often talked about you. He said if Variety ever made a come-back . . .'

'But it has, hasn't it?' Tommy Luton interrupted. Behind the mask of greasepaint the muscles went into a spasm of lugubrious anxiety, the sad beagle-like eyes watered. 'I mean, Mr Saintsbury, it's all happening right here in the clubs. They love me in the clubs.'

'Some talents just never grow old,' said Storer.

'That's true, Arthur,' Tommy Luton agreed feverishly. 'That's very, very true. I was just telling these kids here . . .'

'Staines and Middlecroft,' said one of the young lads. 'Comics.'

'American orientated,' added the other. 'Sophisticated stuff.'

'. . . just telling them,' the old man went on remorselessly, 'what it used to be like in the old days.'

Storer nodded and settled back against the radiator. For a while he would have no need to say anything. The old man would prattle on nostalgically, the pitiful soft sell. In his own good time he would work round to Kathy Arden.

5

When the group came down from the stage Tommy Luton introduced Storer as if he owned him. After that Storer got the old man to take him up to the wings. From behind the spot-light operator Storer took first sight of his victim. Her voice was gentle but she used the microphone well. When she went into a selection of old style ballads she soon had the audience with her, singing along. Storer could not see around the wings but he was aware of them, hundreds out there in the beery darkness, seated at their tables with their pints and ports. The girl coaxed them with inhibited gestures, stiff-elbowed, unconsciously offering up her breasts through the thin shimmering gold material of her dress. The men down there would like that. Luton was whispering in his ear about how successful he would be in London if only he got the chance. Storer winked and nodded as if he was the sharer of a great secret. Tommy's talent was the secret, hidden for fifty-odd years. Luton passed him round the manager and the MC with the same possessiveness, fierce and protective, like a boy showing off a new pup. The racket from the piano was so loud that Storer doubted if any of them even picked up his name. He held on to the curtaining and watched the girl. Some time within the next half hour he might even have to kill her. The thought made the ache in his gut flare up again.

The similarity between her and Rena was uncanny. They might have been twins. Though Rena was the elder by three years, Kathy had the same oval face and green eyes. Her blonde hair was loose-flowing and differently styled but that could be fixed. Her body was the same; long-legged, firm-breasted. Only her movements and expressions were not Rena's. She lacked her sister's brazen self-assurance. Anyone with half an eye could see that Kathy Arden hadn't been in the racket long. With her looks, and a hard-fisted manager behind her, Storer supposed she could have spun out her limited talent and made a small but comfortable career out of it.

Storer's scepticism vanished. Now that he saw Kathy Arden in the flesh he understood how important she was to Rena's plan. A quality of hatred was attached to it; Rena's hatred for the sister she hadn't clapped eyes on for ten years. Kathy was part of the shabby life Rena had left behind. Storer did not believe that the past was a ghost or a devil, or conscience a grisly spectre bent on torturing a man, or a woman, to death. But Storer believed in chance: it was the grimness of chance which he thought of now, the chance which had put Rena in the same place as Rushton, had given her a sister like enough to be a twin, and brought the girl out of a shadowy corner right on cue.

He said, 'She's good.'

Brushing his ragged silk lapels, Tommy Luton said grudgingly, 'Not bad: not bad, *if* you like that kind of thing. Ten-a-penny singers of *her* class, of course. Wouldn't really go down well in the metropolis, if you ask me.'

'Do you know her?'

'No,' Luton said peevishly, adding quickly, 'I'm next on. I can do what she does too, y'know. You watch, I'll really have them eating out of my hand. They know old Tommy Luton here. They like me. Eating out of my hand, in two minutes. You'll see.'

Storer went back to studying the girl again. She looked shy, unused to applause. She had none of the cocksureness which usually stamped a clubland thrush. She looked startled, even as if she had just wakened from a peaceful dream to find herself in front of a raucous mob bent on making her their temporary darling. Until he clamped down on the emotion Storer almost felt sorry for her.

Storer was obliged to take Rena's word for it that the girl was alone in the world. He trusted Rena's efficiency to cover up the disappearance. Kathy Arden was just the type to go missing, to vanish into London and never be heard of again. He thought how he too would die alone; but he was Storer and death was his business. Kathy Arden was too good-looking to die unmourned and unmissed.

She went off on the far side of the stage. Tommy Luton stiffened, his eyes glittering wetly. The youthful MC pranced on; his striped jacket and white ducks might have been fine for the pier at Southport but were out of kilter with a bleak November night in the Midlands. He made a few flattering remarks about Kathy Arden, then, facing the wings, shouted a big welcome back for dear old Tommy Luton.

Luton patted Storer's arm again and said, 'You'll see, Arthur. You watch this.'

As the old man leapt into the blinding light to hollow enthusiasm from the audience, Storer slipped downstairs. He went directly to the females' dressing room and knocked on the door. A plump middle-aged brunette opened it and scowled up at him.

'Miss Arden please.'

'She's dressing.'

'My name,' said Storer, 'is Arthur Saintsbury. I'm an agent.'

'Oh, yer,' said the brunette aggressively. 'I've heard *that* one before.'

'From Radleigh's.'

'What's'at?'

'Radleigh's,' he said. 'Oxford Street.'

'Really!'

'Now look,' Storer said, 'do you give her the message or do I leave? She won't thank you, if you do.'

'Okay,' the girl said. 'Hang on.'

Storer hung on. An occasional gust of restrained laughter drifted down from the stage. He caught the sound of Tommy Luton's shrill voice imploring workers to laugh at him. Storer looked at his watch again. Rena should have the Cortina outside by now. He leaned against the wall and lit a cigarette. He did not want Luton to nail him again. He had had enough of Luton. The dressing-room door opened and he was staring at Kathy Arden.

'Miss Arden,' he said. 'I'm Arthur Saintsbury: Radleigh's theatrical agency, Oxford Street.'

'Yes,' the girl said, puzzled. Storer knew that the brunette was just behind the door.

'Are you represented?'

'What?'

'Do you have an agent?'

'Not exactly,' Kathy said. 'I've . . . a manager. I share a manager.'

'Who?'

'Bill Brentwood.'

'Should I talk to him?' Storer said.

'What about?'

She still had cold cream on her cheek. Storer was tempted to reach forward a finger and wipe it off. He knew it would smell sweet. Perspiration gleamed on her brow where the towel had missed. Her pupils showed how perplexed she was. She looked like Rena, very much like Rena.

'We might be interested in booking you for the Coventry Club,' he lied.

'In London?'

'Yes,' Storer said. 'Where can I find Brentwood?'

'I don't know,' the girl said. She was confused. Storer wanted her confused. She was excited too, but still with wariness behind it.

'*Can* we find him?'

'When – tonight?'

'Our booking opens on Tuesday. I assume you could be in London tomorrow for rehearsals. You're not engaged next week?'

'Bill might be at home,' she said.

'Where's that?'

'Oldham,' the girl said. 'He lives in Oldham. We could telephone.'

'I'd rather talk to him in person.'

'He probably *won't* be at home,' said the girl, 'come to think of it.'

'Why don't we run out there and see?' said Storer.

She was still unsure. If she had been cast in the mould of an actress she would have been able to disguise her mistrust of him, but then she would probably have gone along with him without question, desperate for the chance of a London date.

'I don't have much time,' Storer said. 'If I don't pick up a replacement for the Coventry by tomorrow, my boss will hang me. The regular went down with 'flu. My boss heard about you, and . . .' He paused. 'Look, why don't I go and see this Brentwood chap . . .'

'What if he's not at home,' Kathy Arden said.

Storer shrugged. 'Too bad.'

'You mean . . .'

'I'll look elsewhere,' Storer said. 'I'm sorry, but it's urgent. You know how it is.'

She tossed her head a little, making her breasts rise boldly. Storer did not look at them, keeping his eyes on her eyes.

'All right,' she said. 'I know some other places Bill might be. I suppose it's too good a chance to pass up.'

'Get your belongings,' Storer said, 'and let's go.'

'Shan't be a moment,' the girl said.

Now she had committed herself she was as eager as any tuppenny thrush who had just glimpsed the starlight of the big time. Storer felt sorry for her again: he held the emotion while he waited. He could hear the brunette muttering behind the door: was she warning Kathy off, or encouraging her?

The audience chuckled, salting appreciation with a couple of derisive hoots. Luton shouted at them. The off-key piano started, hesitated, waiting for the aged trouper to pick up the tune: 'Lily of Laguna'. Storer blinked. The girl came out and it wasn't Kathy Arden any longer, it was Rena Rushton. With her long hair tucked up in a scarlet beret and the coat buttoned to the throat she was Rena's double.

'I hope,' said the brunette, 'you know what you're doing?'

'Taking my chance,' Kathy Arden said.

She tossed her head again, and pulled the bag up under her arm. Storer ushered her down the corridor ahead of him. When he turned the brunette was still scowling at him; he decided she was less suspicious than envious, and gave her a derisive wave. She slammed the dressing-room door.

He took Kathy past the piles of empty crates into the yard.

'My car's round the corner,' he said, pointing. 'That way.'

She nodded nervously.

Storer prayed that Rena had got through on time. She had: the Cortina, with the lights out, was pulled over into the shelter of the gable. He glanced behind him, then took his right hand from his pocket and clipped Kathy with the base of his palm just below the ear. She gave a little grunt and began to go down. He stepped up and caught her, catching the bag too, and hurried her forward to the Cortina. He opened the rear near-side door and pushed her in, bundling her across the seat.

Rena stared round at him and took off the ridiculous dark glasses.

'Is she dead?'

'No,' Storer said.

He strode round to the driver's side and ordered the woman to move over.

'I want you to kill her, Storer,' Rena snapped. 'I want her dead.'

'Shut up,' Storer said.

He started the car and nosed it out between the sides of the buses, carefully negotiating the ranks of parked cars. Beside him Rena craned over the back of the seat, inspecting her sister's unconscious features.

'She is like me, isn't she?' Rena said.

'Yes,' said Storer. 'Quite.'

He felt the kerb under the front wheels and turned the car slowly into the roadway. Then he pressed down on the gas. He had left his raincoat hanging in the dressing room, but it didn't matter. The gun was in his jacket pocket and there was nothing in the coat to give away his identity.

'I don't want her to see me, Storer,' Rena was saying.

'She won't.'

'What happens when she comes round?'

'I'll kill her if I have to,' Storer said. 'That was the deal.'

6

It took Storer ten minutes to pack his belongings, and pay his bill at the desk of the Grosvenor. From a call-box round the corner Rena Rushton telephoned an

Oldham number. She explained to Bill Brentwood that she, Kathy Arden, had been offered a spot in London and would not be returning to the Midland scene. At first Brentwood was astonished. Then he was anxious to cut in on her engagement. He could only dimly remember what she sounded like as a singer but had no trouble in recalling her appearance. He had even thought of trying a little additional promotion of his own at night, but with two star-struck dollies currently sharing his bed he had decided to hold off. Brentwood did not imagine that Kathy Arden would be going anywhere, least of all London. She sounded a little different tonight, harder. Perhaps two months of casual club dates had toughened her and skimmed off the innocence which he had noticed when he took her on. He kicked himself for having failed to give her more of his time and attention. With no signed contract any smart agent would be able to carve him out. He didn't own her. Life was full of lost opportunities, and he had other singers, better singers than Kathy Arden, even if she was a looker. He sighed, wished her luck and hung up the phone.

When Rena got back to the car Storer was already in the driving seat. He had arranged the girl in the back seat under an overcoat. She looked like a drunk sleeping it off. Her face didn't show at all and he had pulled her into a foetal position so that any passing cop who happened to glance in would have nothing to remember, except perhaps a glimpse of the long attractive legs. Storer steered the Cortina out of Manchester on to the Stockport road. It was still raining, driving in now against the windscreen. The wipers worked rhythmically as the dreary towns flew by. He drove for an hour and a half without opening his mouth.

Rena smothered her anger at his silence. She was afraid of losing him: she needed him to do the things which she could not do alone and which, at this stage, no one else would dare do. She wanted to talk to him, rage at him, but his silence intimidated her. She said nothing. He did not look at her, keeping the dark burnt-out eyes fixed on the sweeping roadway ahead, the fists low on the wheel. Suddenly he spoke.

'Listen,' he said, 'the thinking's all wrong.'

'You agreed,' she said.

'Sure,' said Storer, 'but I should have thought it through more carefully.'

'Don't you think she can pass for me?'

'Under certain circumstances,' Storer said carefully. 'But she's more useful to us alive.'

'You're afraid to kill her,' Rena said accusingly.

'I'll kill her when the time's ripe,' Storer said. 'But first we've got to manufacture the right circumstances and it's going to be twice as difficult when she's dead.'

'I thought you . . .'

'Listen,' said Storer again. 'If you want me to kill her, I will, but the rest of the deal will go bust.'

'I dress her in my clothes . . .'

'Run her over and leave her, covered in identification,' said Storer. 'Sure, but I don't know if a coroner will buy it.'

'There needn't be an inquest,' the woman said. 'Rushton *knows* you're going to kill me. He's paying you to do it. Do you think he's going to demand . . .?'

'Rushton has nothing to do with it,' said Storer. 'An inquest is one thing we can't risk. What he wants most is the briefcase.'

'Was he really frightened?'

'Worried,' said Storer. 'So would you be if someone

ran off with your private accounts. He was crazy to keep them in one place, especially with you around. He knows you're going to blackmail him. His real worry is that you're not in it alone.'

'I'm going to take him for every penny I can,' Rena said.

'Suits me,' said Storer.

'But I don't want to die in the process,' Rena said.

She had put on the tinted spectacles again. Storer could not tell if there was a glint of fear in her eyes or not. He supposed there was: nobody liked the idea of dying. He wondered at the greed which had fertilised this scheme in her brain. Perhaps she had discovered just how little honest money Rushton owned. She only married him to become a widow, but the organisation was so knit that she would be lucky to come out with a handful of good stones and a wardrobe full of clothes. She wouldn't be the first hustler to live high on the hog as a rich man's wife only to fall foul of the law and the deviousness of her husband's transactions when he left her to widowhood. On rough estimate Storer reckoned she would clear around fifty thousand: for Rena that obviously wasn't enough. Better the big gamble on a quarter of a million now than a small slice of pie in ten or fifteen years. Rushton had partners who wouldn't like the empire divvied up just to keep a fancy widow in luxury for the rest of her life. Widows, especially widows as sharp and avaricious as Rena, were dangerous to the financial structure.

She had promised him fifty thousand pounds. With that much in his pocket he could quit. He knew a couple of accountants who would spread the stake in foreign banks. He could then live clear in any country which took his fancy, leave London and the trade in death behind. He had been one of the shroud society for too long.

He said, 'Why blow your passport?'

'I don't understand,' Rena said. 'I told you my plan and you agreed to it. If Rushton takes her for me then I'm in the clear. I can bleed him forever and he'll never think to look for me. I'll be dead.'

'Squeeze him first,' said Storer.

'And what do we do with her?' Rena said. 'She's a whining little bitch. She won't want any part of it. As far as she's concerned she has no sister. She hasn't changed, I'll bet. She's still Mummy's little girl, even if Mummy's under the ground, and little Kathy, good little Kathy's all alone in the world.'

'I'm not interested in your psychological problems,' Storer said. 'I'm only interested in doing the job right.'

'You don't want to kill her?'

'Not yet,' said Storer. 'First of all you get that briefcase and . . .'

'You must think I'm crazy. I don't trust you, Storer – or Rushton. I've been married to him for two years. Even if he does stick me off in the background I've heard enough to tell me that he's not an easy man to fool. Provided he doesn't know where that case is, then I'll stay alive. Even you won't kill me until you know where it is. That briefcase is my life-line.'

'I'm on your side, remember,' said Storer.

'You're on your own side, Storer,' said Rena. 'I wouldn't put it past you to grab the case and put the bite on him yourself.'

'I wouldn't buck the syndicate,' Storer said. 'I don't have that much nerve.'

'Look, Storer, the original plan was to give Rushton my corpse . . .'

'What we'll do now,' said Storer, 'is keep the girl on ice . . .'

'I don't want her to see me.'

'That can be arranged,' Storer said. 'Keep her on ice, while I pretend to chase around looking for you. Meanwhile you start soaking Rushton. Are you sure he'll pay for what you have in that case?'

'He'll pay,' Rena said. 'He'll pay all right.'

'Then after a couple of weeks I kill you – not you, but your sister. I can do it with a couple of Rushton's extras on the spot so there'll be no questions asked. She'll be dressed in your clothes and carrying your identification. You don't mind losing some of your jewellery, do you?'

'Some of the poorer stuff, no.'

'Then after she's dead – *you're* dead – you put the final screw in Rushton and we split and run. Simple.'

'Complicated,' Rena said. 'And dangerous.'

'It's a dangerous game whichever way you play it,' Storer said.

'How do you propose keeping her on ice for two weeks without tipping our hand?'

'Leave that to me,' Storer said.

'Storer,' Rena said. 'Do you want her?'

'God, no,' Storer said. He laughed, low in his throat. 'What's the point of having her when I've already got you? Same thing, isn't it?'

'No, it's not,' Rena said. 'It's not the same thing at all.'

'All I want,' said Storer, 'is my money.'

'I believe you,' Rena said.

Behind them the girl on the seat groaned and whimpered. Rena stared at him with a kind of smug triumph. 'Now what?'

Storer stopped the car by the roadside, got out and

went to the back. He opened the door and leaning inside lifted the girl's face up between finger and thumb. Her skin was as pale as milk and her eyelids a bluish colour. She was breathing high, struggling to gather the consciousness she needed to bring herself round. Storer sighed and clipped her deftly behind the ear again.

'If you do that often enough you will kill her,' Rena said.

Storer lowered the girl to the seat and made her comfortable beneath the coat. 'Never,' he said. 'I've never killed anyone that way yet.'

He returned to the driving seat and set the hired Cortina off on the road to London.

'That should hold her,' he said, almost to himself, 'until we arrive.'

'Arrive where?' Rena asked.

'Watford,' Storer said. 'I've a friend there who'll look after her until we need her.'

'A friend,' Rena said acidly. 'I didn't know you had any.'

'One or two,' Storer lied.

'I just hope you can trust him.'

'I can trust this one,' Storer said softly. 'This one's my mother.'

7

'Ay, so it's yourself, is it?' the big woman said. 'And not before time either.' She opened the back door for him and Storer crossed the threshold into the kitchen. 'Some time of night this t'be dropping in.'

She was dressed in a shapeless dressing-gown beneath which Storer could see the hem of a flannel nightdress moulded to massive bare calves. Her hair was crimped in metal curlers and she looked just as he always remembered her, big and ugly and untidy. The kitchen was in its usual state of disorder; dishes piled in the sink, unwashed clothing everywhere, a regiment of milk bottles down the side of the greasy gas-stove. The smell was the same too, stale and warm. The whole cramped little house smelled like an unmade bed. Storer was home again.

Agnes MacAusland was no blood kin to Storer but she was the only mother he could really remember. His parents had separated a year after his birth in the depths of a Gorbals slum in Glasgow. He had been 'temporarily' farmed out to the childless couple next door. Later when his real mother was buried in the ruins of Clydebank in the blitz of 1941 he had stayed on with the MacAuslands. They moved to Watford when he was eight and he went with them. It was Alex MacAusland who set the lad's feet on the paths of wickedness but Storer did not hold it against him. Alex had died of a complicated bronchial disease twelve years ago. He left young Storer nothing but a few minor contacts in the underworld, and an education in the methods of petty theft. Soon after, being the breadwinner, Storer cleared out of the Watford house. Since then he had returned only a dozen times, dropping in out of the blue. Once every six months, however, as regular as an almanacked event, he slipped a sheaf of bank notes into a registered envelope and sent it to the woman who had reared him. Part of his reason for breaking contact with her was his fear that she would draw the attention of one of the men who hated him, and become the victim of reprisals. He had no desire to involve her in his life, though he was closer to her than to any other person. If she guessed the truth, she still could not prevent herself chiding him with neglect. Of the bi-annual gift of money, which kept her alive and in squalid comfort, she said nothing; never had. How she spent the money, what she did for company or amusement, Storer neither knew nor cared. Ma MacAusland was a hard-bitten independent Scot and would not have welcomed his concern with her welfare. He supported her and that was as much interference as her pride would allow.

'D'y'want something to eat?'

'Scrambled eggs,' Storer said. 'And coffee.'

'Away in an' sit down. I'll make it,' she said. She nodded towards the living-room, but Storer lingered with her in the cluttered kitchen.

'Make it for two,' he said.

'I'm not hungry,' she said. 'I just woke up.'

'I've somebody with me.'

'Have y'now?'

'Outside in the car.'

'Better bring him in then, eh, before he freezes t'death.'

'It's a woman,' Storer said.

She glowered at him, and clattered pots in the sink, searching for one a little cleaner than the rest. 'A woman is it? Somebody special?'

'Not in the way you mean,' Storer said. He pulled a chair from under the table, swept off a tangle of soiled clothes and straddled it. The woman found eggs in the cupboard and brought them to the sink and broke them, spilling albumen on the front of her robe. 'But she is special.'

'Bring her in then,' the woman said.

'Not yet,' Storer said. 'Listen, Ma. I want you to do me a large favour.'

'What's that?'

'I want you to look after a girl for a while.'

'I don't take lodgers.'

'Not as a lodger,' Storer said. 'As a prisoner. Keep her here for a couple of weeks, feed her and look after her but most of all make sure she doesn't escape.'

Ma MacAusland turned to face her foster-son, the beater poised in one hand, the bowl in the other. 'Why should I?'

'I've never asked you to do anything before,' Storer said. He picked his words carefully. 'I've no one else to turn to. I can't trust anyone in the city. Remember what Alex used to say – never trust anybody you can buy: well, I only know people you can buy.'

'Don't you think you've bought me?'

'No,' said Storer. 'I couldn't buy you with the Koh-i-Noor diamond.'

'Supposin' I turn you down?'

'Nothing will change,' Storer said. He shook his head. 'No blackmail with you, Ma.'

'Tell me about the girl.'

Whipping the egg mess, the bowl cradled in the crook of her elbow, she listened while he told her a little of the story, just enough to let her see how important it was to him. He did not tell her about the briefcase or wanting the girl killed, just that he was working on a job and needed a prison for the girl for a while.

'You've got that back room, the one without the window,' he said. 'It'll be perfect.'

'An' what about sanitation?'

'Yeah,' Storer said. 'You can go with her.'

'Uh! She'll not care for that much.'

'She'll not care much for any of it,' Storer said. 'She'll be . . . scared to death, but you can calm her down. Feed her up and calm her down and just make sure she doesn't get out. In the long run it's for her own good.'

'How bad trouble are you in, Storer?'

'It's of my own making,' Storer said. 'I'm still in control, but I've got to work to keep it that way.'

'An' what if you don't then?'

'It's a hard life,' Storer said, quietly.

'The chop?'

'Possibly,' he said.

'I'll take her,' the woman said. The beater clopped round the bowl for a while longer, then she put it aside and poured the yellow fluid into the pot. Wiping her hands on the skirt of the robe, she said, 'She won't get away from me.'

'I'll pay you, of course,' Storer said.

'Ay, lad,' said the woman, grinning, 'bloody right you will. Now go and bring in the lassie and we'll get everything settled.'

'Sure,' Storer said. 'Thanks, Ma.'

'It's the least I can do,' she said. 'Anyway, Storer, I wouldn't want you dead.'

'No?'

'Them parcels might stop,' she said. 'Then where would I be?'

Storer shook his head ruefully and went out of the kitchen to fetch the sisters.

7

'Is she really your mother?' Rena asked.

'Yeah,' Storer replied.

'Funny, I never thought of you as anybody's son.'

'Did you think I was born old?' said Storer.

'I'm glad I don't have to stay there,' Rena said. 'Kathy'll never get away from your mother. She's as tough as you are.'

'I know,' Storer said.

'I suppose you didn't tell your mother what we intend to do to her?'

'No,' Storer said.

Rena laughed. 'Is this the first time you've ever brought a girl home?'

Storer did not reply.

Rena said, 'She didn't take much to me.'

'Forget it,' Storer said, harshly.

'You're tired?'

'Yeah.'

He was tired. He badly wanted sleep: not just sleep itself, but time to lie before he went over, and the cool lucid period when he wakened, to think out his course of action. Kathy Arden was still alive and Rena still had the briefcase. If he wanted to bring sudden pressure on Rushton he would have to move fast. He trusted Ma MacAusland but even she, sixty now, was not infallible. If the girl did manage to get away then the whole scheme would be shot. It could happen. It was not a stable situation, but it was a damned sight better than Rena's original plan. It would surely have precipitated them into a long-odds gamble of a kind Storer preferred to avoid. Rena would put the bite on Rushton and in turn Rushton would put the bite on him. But not until money was flowing freely would he turn up with Rena's corpse. If he could lay hands on the contents of the briefcase, he might not have to kill Kathy Arden at all. At the moment, though, he could see no way around it. If he released her she would be sure to scream to the cops: the last thing he wanted was trouble with the law. It would finish him with Rushton and Rena, and end his run of luck as far as England was concerned. Once they got on to him, he would have no alternative but to fade from the scene. Sooner or later Kathy Arden would have to die.

'I know what you need,' Rena said.

The first flush of morning traffic was heading into the city, lorries laden with market produce, the cars of council employees starting up early, the dregs of Sunday's revellers crawling back to another week of money-making. The rain had gone off now and pre-dawn mists hung over the parks. About now Kathy Arden would be coming out of her blackness into fear and bewilderment in strange surroundings. Ma would handle her, firmly but gently. He did not think Kathy would cause much trouble: there seemed to be so little violence in her. Yet she must share with Rena some of the caustic intelligence which the elder sister showed.

'Where did your sister live?' he asked.

'Don't worry about that,' Rena said. 'I'll fix it.'

'In digs?'

'I'll send her landlady money and have her forward the belongings.'

'How did you find out?' Storer asked suddenly. 'I thought you were in it alone.'

'You're tired, Storer,' Rena said.

'Answer my question, Rena,' he said. 'Is there somebody else?'

'*My* one trusted friend,' the woman said. 'And I *don't* mean my mother.'

'Do they have the briefcase?'

'They might,' Rena said.

She would tell him no more. While he parked the hired Cortina she went into the Gresham nearby. It was not daylight yet, but it was not night either. It was no-man's time, a dead period between night and day, between one week and the next. Storer went quietly up to his room. In the dining-room below somebody was up and about already. He could hear the clink of crockery. He hung the *Do Not Disturb* notice on the door, slipped off his shoes and lay down on the bed. He had too much to think about to sleep, but he rested, motionless, breathing shallowly.

On the floor above Rena would be waiting for him. He felt no desire for her now. He did not go up to her but he did not sleep.

At eighty-thirty he got up and made himself ready for another day. At nine, with a Gresham breakfast inside him, he felt better and even whistled a little tune to himself as he walked round to Wilcox Square to pick up the Porsche. He could have been any successful young man off to boost his bank balance with a hard day's work at the office. But he wasn't. He was Storer and his cheerfulness was only skin deep.

Part Two

1

Kathy came slowly out of nightmarish darkness. Pain flickered behind her eyes; they burned with it, sending spear-like flames across her face and down into her throat. She drew up her knees, moved wooden arms and crushed the pain with her fists. Something took her and shifted her hands. She felt coldness against her skin. She sucked in breath. The coldness came again and again until the shock of it turned to soothing ease. She opened her eyes. In the minute's balancing between reality and dream she half expected to see her mother bent over her. But the woman was not her mother. Her mother had been gaunt and sallow and small; this woman was ruddy-skinned and massive. A hand came out and gently lifted her face towards the bosom of the robe and the cold pressed against her ear again, soothing. The woman's mouth, when next she saw it, was firm and unyielding.

'Who are you?'

'Call me Ma,' the woman said. She held the girl down against the blanket with her forearm and squeezed out the lint pad. Water trickled into a yellow baking bowl on a chair by the bedside.

Kathy struggled. 'What are you doing to me? Where . . .?'

'Shush,' the woman said. 'Don't fash yourself, m'dear. You'll be all right.'

It was not a hospital. It was not her room in Manchester. It was nowhere she had been before and this woman was no one she knew. She was lost, totally lost, submerged under a wave of panic. She tried to piece it all together but could get no further than the stage of the Winfield Club, light shining, bright and dazzling in her eyes. The woman leaned over her, blotting out the room. Kathy inched her mind past the faces which floated in the tide of darkness, pale and uniform as a shoal of jellyfish. She remembered the man: not his name, but the height of him, his aggressive politeness and authority. She remembered Elaine in the dressing room, the promise of the London job, going down the corridor into the damp night air. Nothing after that: nothing at all: blank.

'Tell me where I am, *please*.'

'In safe keeping,' the woman said.

She allowed Kathy to rise, propping her with an arm, and let her survey the room. There were no windows. It was as small as a cell, but not bare. It was cluttered with all sorts of junk, like the back room of a market stall – a heavy dresser, a table, chairs, cardboard boxes jagged with vases and brass candlesticks and cheap china ornaments, bundles of yellowing magazines and tattered books, all shrouded in a thin grey dust. Even the bed on which she lay had a gritty feeling, and smelled musty like a dungeon. The man must have something to do with it. She explored her body and its sensations, but seemed to have suffered no indignity and, with relief, lay back and fought down her fear. The woman's expression might be shuttered and barred like an oaken door but her manner and actions were kindly. In the grey eyes, Kathy imagined she could see sympathy. That she needed sympathy at all was sufficient warning that she was in danger: some of her terror returned.

In the palm the two flat white pills looked like aspirin. The woman thrust them at her, the glass in the other hand. Kathy took the pills and put them in her mouth. They were bitter and she swallowed them quickly, even though she suspected that they were not aspirin but something else. Drugs? Almost immediately the pain behind her eyeballs began to subside and she felt tension sliding out of her. Her head rolled.

The woman said, 'Listen, m'dear, you'll be here for a wee while. But you and me, we'll get along just fine, provided you do what you're told.'

'Why?'

'Reasons are none of our business,' the woman said. 'Now there's nothin' to fret about. You'll be safe with me, if you stick to the rules.'

'Why?'

'I can't tell you why because I don't know,' the woman said. 'My instructions are to keep you safe here, an' that's all.'

'Here?'

'In this room,' the woman said. 'You'll be fed and cared for, and no harm will come to you, but for the time being you're my prisoner. Ay, it's a harsh word, but it's the right one. You're the prisoner and I'm the guard.'

'But . . . why me? I'm not . . . important to anyone.'

'Ay, but you are,' the woman said. 'From what I gather you're very important.' She put her hand on Kathy's brow and lifted back the fringe of blonde hair. 'Take comfort in that. You mean a lot to somebody.'

'I'm . . . frightened.'

'It's natural,' the woman said. 'No need t'be frightened of me though. I'll look after you. You'll be safe enough here.' She picked up the bowl and glass and stepped back. Her shadow was as solid and huge as that of a mountain with sunlight behind it. Festooned in dust the naked bulb was a tiny muted sun fading to twilight. Kathy blinked and struggled ineffectually against sleep. '. . . safe enough here, provided you don't try to escape.'

Then the woman was gone and she was alone, lying immobilised on her back, staring up at the bulb. In the instant before sleep claimed her she heard the lock click loudly in the dusty silence. She knew she was trapped. Then questions and fear melted and the bulb dimmed out to total darkness. The drug took full effect.

2

In the morning Storer made the rounds of the addresses on Rushton's list. It should have taken him longer, would have too if he had been setting out to find the woman. As a token gesture, however, it was sufficient. Undoubtedly Rushton had sent out feelers, and Storer was only concerned with making himself look stupid. First he checked off the department store accounts, then the beauticians and a couple of restaurants. Around one o'clock he ate soup in a café off Shaftesbury Avenue, and smoked and thought while the sixpence in the meter ran out. Then he took the Porsche across the river into Lambeth.

A chill sun had struggled out of the winter haze and

cast its feeble rays down on the cupola of the War Museum, making it gleam dully like a crust of arctic sea-ice. Blocks of council flats rose stark against the canvas sky, brick weathered to the dun of autumn as if even buildings here camouflaged themselves for the long winter. The metal frames of the windows and doors looked frost-bound and the glass was opaque with the back-sheen of fluorescent strip-lighting. Storer left the car at the kerb in Brankscombe Row and crossed the outfield under the towering block to the entrance door. He fished a diary from his pocket and turned to the back where a coded name and address was written. He checked the number in the diary with the block number fixed to the brick, entered the building and took the elevator to the tenth floor. Though he had never been in prison, he had seen enough movies to give him a picture of the American jail system, and the corridors of the flats chimed an echo of that impression in his mind. After a couple of wrong turnings he found what he wanted: Griggs even had his name on the door. Storer rang the bell.

Over the sag of the guard-chain a section of Griggs's face appeared. Storer had to look down at it. The face was grizzled with salt-and-pepper stubble and the mouth had collapsed toothlessly in on itself. The eyes were the colour of concrete chips.

'Oh, God, Storer, can't you leave me alone?'

Storer put his fist out quickly and set it square between door and jamb so that Griggs could not close the door on him without smashing his hand. He knew that Griggs would not dare damage him and kept the hand there, while Griggs jogged about beneath it, glaring up at him.

'I've retired, Storer. I've chucked it. I'm out. Now

bugger off and leave me in peace, will yer?'

'Henry,' Storer said amiably. 'You've got it all wrong.'

'Go on, bugger off.'

'Hen-ry.' Storer reached into his left breast pocket with his right hand. Griggs darted out of sight, and Storer felt the pressure of the door on his closed fist. He extended his right arm through the crack, wriggling it until the chain came tight. He waved the notes like a fan. 'Hen-ry.'

Sullenly Griggs unlatched the hook. The chain fell away and Storer entered the flat.

Griggs looked not only old but ill, as if the wastage of alcohol in his system had given way to less pure diseases. He stank of decay. The freshly washed and ironed shirt which he wore still carried the faint imprints of black sweat under each armpit. His little body had been stripped down to a collection of bones; only the unhealthy paunch bulging against the leather belt which held up his patched corduroys gave him any substance at all. Wisps of hair stood up from the backs of his ears like burned grass.

'Are you alone?'

'Yer, the missus is out.'

'Put your teeth in, Henry,' Storer said, 'and let's talk.'

Griggs looked at the bank-notes as they went up and vanished into Storer's pocket again. He ran his tongue over his caved-in lips. It was a blunt short tongue like a budgerigar's. He jerked his hand. 'In there.'

The living-room had a pleasant view over the park. The sun had gone now and in the early dusk the lights of the hospital in the middle distance made bleak orderly patterns. There were few people about; those that were moved pointlessly and ant-like on the pavements and squares below. Storer could see the red roof of the Porsche, like a match-box toy laid against the graceful curve of the kerb. There was nothing much in the room; a plastic-covered lounge suite, a television set. A book-case, knocked together by a handyman who wasn't, was lined with paperbacks. A trolley supported an ugly china lamp. One bar of the wall heater was lit, but otherwise the room was in shadow. Griggs came in from the bathroom with his teeth back in his head. He switched on the lamp and slumped down wearily in the small armchair beneath it. He lifted the ten-packet of Gold Flake from the trolley and poked it out at Storer. Storer shook his head, watched Griggs light the cigarette and draw the smoke down into him greedily and with a contused rasping sound, as if it had to filter through a long wet sponge to reach an area where it could be felt. Storer had watched Alex MacAusland go in much the same way. He waited for Griggs to cough but he didn't.

'How's Ma MacAusland?' Griggs asked.

'Fine,' said Storer.

'Give 'er my love when you see 'er next.'

'I will,' Storer said. 'How long have you got?'

'Eh?'

'How long have the quacks given you, Henry?'

'Quacks,' said Griggs. 'They're sly buggers you know. Won't even admit it's all up with me. But the missus and me know all right.'

'How long?'

Griggs shrugged and even that effort seemed to tire him. He fiddled with the stud in the throat of the collarless shirt. 'Who knows?' he said. 'Sometimes I think the quicker the better. If it wasn't for Martha I wouldn't even mind.' He chuckled painfully. 'Might even speed up the process myself.'

'Can you do a job?'

Griggs shook his head. 'Can't even let a man die in peace, Storer, can you? I'm no use to you now, son. I'm finished. I can't wipe me bum unaided.'

'You've still got your contacts,' Storer said.

Griggs lowered himself back in the armchair and crossed his short stick-brittle legs at the ankles. 'What do you need that you can't get yourself?'

'Information.'

'And what can I get in return that'd be any use to me now?'

'Money.'

'Money!' said Griggs scornfully. 'What do I need money for?'

'Your missus,' Storer said. 'I don't suppose you've got a fortune tucked away.'

In the dying light Griggs's eyes took on a brief gleam as if they had not been concrete at all but dusty marble and somehow Storer had blown that dust away. It was the glint of greed all right but of a kind Storer had never known before, a rare variety.

Storer said, 'I'll give you fifty.'

'A hundred.'

'Seventy-five.'

'A hundred.'

'All right,' said Storer. 'But it better be worth it.'

'Tell me,' Griggs said, 'exactly what you want to know.'

'Rena Rushton,' Storer said.

Griggs smiled. 'She's missing.'

'I know that,' Storer said. 'I want a list of her contacts.'

'What can I find out that Rushton can't?' said Griggs.

'Knowing you, Henry, I'd say plenty.'

'Are you doing this behind Rushton's back?' said Griggs. ' 'Cause if you are I want no part of it. I got troubles enough.'

'It's sanctioned,' said Storer. 'But listen, I'm not interested in finding out where she is, I just want background. You know, shake the skeletons out of her cupboard.'

'Not easy,' said Griggs. 'She must've known thousands of men before she got 'er hooks in Rushton.'

'Well,' said Storer, 'if anyone can dig up what I want, you can, Henry. Alex always said you were the best in the business.'

'Yer, but I haven't flown in years,' Griggs replied.

'Better to fall from the air,' Storer said, 'than die on the ground.'

'Better not to die at all,' Griggs said. He lifted his shoulders again, staring into the twisting heat of the radiator. 'But it's too late to stop it.'

'Nobody can,' Storer said. 'Take comfort in that.'

'Storer,' Griggs said. 'How big is this caper?'

'Big.'

'I hope I last out.'

'You will,' Storer said, adding soundlessly under his breath, 'God willing.'

3

Rushton's London home was a small but luxurious suite of rooms above the Stag's Palace in the triangle of Soho which lies near St Giles. The narrow facia of the club was almost painfully discreet and the decor had a tastefulness which suggested that a hand other than Rushton's had designed it. The suite was done out in plain wood and crafty fabrics into which the ox-hide sofas and armchairs fitted discreetly. The Stag's Palace was a masculine club and the rooms above it were masculine too, with no trace of the aggressive overstatements which rob some big-time joints of individuality. Serious gamblers filled the places at the tables: women were kept apart, relegated to anterooms, classed in the same bracket as good food and excellent wine. Gambling was a business, the other services offered respite and refreshment which only the rich and the lucky could afford. Storer had phoned ahead and consequently had no trouble obtaining admission. But he was steered clear of the tables, led by a backstairs route like a servant, to the upper rooms.

Rushton had just finished dining and the remains of the meal lay on a silver tray on a side table, coffee pot and brandy glass on the desk beside him. Desks were a dominant feature of Rushton's life and none of his residences was without one. Viewing the world from behind an expanse of leather-trimmed oak added to the boss's sense of security, Storer supposed; perhaps he just liked having something solid on which to lean his elbows.

'I haven't found her,' Storer said. 'Not a trace.'

'I know,' Rushton said. He took a sip of Turkish

coffee followed by a sip of brandy. He was without a jacket. The snug waistcoat over the white shirt, and the fancy armbands, gave him the appearance of an American cattle baron. His dark tie was loose and flowing. He tucked it deeper into the V of the waistcoat, plucking and fussing with it while he spoke. 'I'm beginning to wonder if you're really the man for the job.'

'I've still a few irons in the fire,' Storer said, 'I expect something to break soon.'

'Something has,' Rushton said.

'Oh?' said Storer. He helped himself to one of the cigarettes in the glass on the desk and lit it casually from the lighter. 'What?'

'This,' said Rushton. He shook out the buff-coloured telegram like a conjurer producing a snake from his sleeve. 'This, this.'

Storer took the telegram.

It said – PREPARE FIRST PAYMENT STOP OPEN ON TWENTY-FIVE STOP CHARITY WILL BE DESIGNATED WEDNESDAY STOP LOVE RENA STOP.

'I'm not surprised,' Storer said. 'But she got off her mark faster than I anticipated.'

'Somebody's in it with her,' said Rushton.

'Perhaps your wife is already dead,' Storer suggested. He thought the idea might be new to Rushton but apparently not. The boss nodded his agreement.

'Could be,' he said. 'That would make things even more difficult.'

'Do you still want me to kill her – if I find her?'

'Yes, Storer.'

'You might destroy any lead you have to the briefcase,' Storer pointed out.

He could see that Rena's treachery had affected

Rushton deeply, though the boss was careful not to show it too obviously. The ancient decree of honour was being invoked: Rushton would adhere to the code. If Rena had cheated on him sexually he might have forgiven her, but she had struck at the stability of his empire, the equivalent of sticking a dagger in his heart. She had betrayed him and made him appear foolish in front of the other members of the syndicate. If they did not know of the threat just yet they would soon have to be told. At his age and in his position loss of face was serious for Rushton.

Storer said, 'How did she lift the case anyway?'

Rushton snorted. 'She took it from the back of my car.'

'Which car?'

'The Mercedes,' said Rushton. 'What's that got to do with it?'

Storer blinked. 'Wasn't it locked?'

'Yes, it was locked. It locks automatically,' said Rushton. 'The Mercedes is practically impregnable.'

'Where was the car?'

'Outside my house in Crumlington,' Rushton said. He looked at Storer then drove himself on, speaking in a flat hard factual tone which warned Storer not to laugh at him. Storer would not have laughed at him anyway, but Rushton was afraid even of silent mockery.

'I had the . . . contents of the case taken out of my safe . . .'

'By whom?'

'Me,' said Burchill from a corner.

'Roy filled the case and put it in the Mercedes, then the telephone rang and I answered it. Roy came in to the house to pick up my overnight bag. We were indoors about ten minutes. When we came out again, together, the door of the Mercedes was open and the briefcase was gone. My wife was gone too.'

'In her own car?'

'Yes – a Ventora.'

'Was the door of the Mercedes forced?' Storer asked.

'No. It seemed to have been unlocked. Naturally it wouldn't be difficult for Rena to forge a key.'

'She only had ten minutes' start,' said Storer. 'Couldn't you run her down?'

'Crumlington's a small place,' said Rushton, 'but it opens out on to four highways and . . . well, I suppose we picked the wrong one.'

'No sign of the Ventora?'

'None. I've circulated dealers and garages, but it's obvious she's holed up some place and has the car with her.'

'Where was the telegram sent from?' asked Storer.

'Lambeth,' said Rushton. 'Lambeth of all places. We don't know anyone in Lambeth. It's not our territory any more. Look here, Storer, do you have a lead; any sort of a lead?'

'A little one,' said Storer. 'It might come to naught.'

'She's not alone in this,' said Rushton again. He waved the offending telegram. 'Look how she signs herself, the bitch – Love Rena. I ask you, Storer, what kind of a lousy joke is that? Love! She hates me. After all I've given her, she still hates me. I dragged her out of a deadbeat show where she didn't even have her own spot. I didn't just pay her and climb aboard; no, I treated her with respect. I treated her with the greatest kind of respect a man can show a woman – I married her. Now look what the whore does to me.'

He jerked up the brandy and spilled some over his silk tie. Storer, embarrassed and silent, watched the liquor sink into the dark fabric.

'She's not alone in this,' Rushton went on. 'She couldn't dream all this up by herself.' He calmed himself, cradling the bulb of the glass in his hands and staring down into it as if it was a crystal ball. His voice was soft and sibilant. 'But she went along with it. She went all the way with it. There's no real stink of coercion, Storer. I've no use for traitors and greedy bitches who take me for a ride. I want her killed, Storer.'

'And you want the briefcase back?'

'Yes.'

'In the meantime are you going to pay up?'

'Twenty-five thousand,' said Rushton sadly. He finished the brandy and started on the coffee. He drank down two small cupfuls before he replied. 'It depends on the pitch.'

'I'm not prying,' Storer said, 'but if the contents of that case can take you into court maybe you'd better play ball for a while.'

'I hate it,' Rushton said. 'I hate it and her and the whole stinking thing.'

Storer stubbed his cigarette in the ash-tray and cleared his throat. 'Piecemeal,' Storer said. 'It might be a piecemeal transaction. Is that possible? She might sell you a sheet at a time.'

'It's possible,' Rushton said. 'The taxman would just love copies of those accounts.'

'If you don't cooperate,' Storer said, 'she may ship them to the Revenue one sheet at a time. No bluff about it, one sheet at a time until you learn sense and pay up.'

'It's true,' Rushton said. 'Too damn' true.'

'I need a man,' Storer said, 'on call. You want it done by Wednesday. I've got to work fast out of nothing. Let me know if and when the instructions come. If I were you, Mr Rushton, I'd have the cash on hand.'

'Whose side are you on, Storer?'

'We might be able to pick up a lead at the dropping point,' Storer said. 'Assuming we haven't found her by then.'

'You don't sound hopeful,' Rushton said. 'I thought you were a bright boy.'

'I am a bright boy,' Storer said. 'I'm also a realist. You and I both know you've asked me to do the impossible.' He got up. 'That always takes a little longer, doesn't it?'

'A man on call,' Rushton said. 'All right, Storer. Anyone in particular.'

'Burchill will do,' Storer said, without hesitation. 'You know you can trust him.'

Rushton thought it over, then nodded.

'Roy,' Rushton called. Storer did not turn round to look at the man in the corner. 'Roy, when Storer calls . . .'

'I jump,' said Burchill coldly. 'Yes, sir, I jump.'

4

'Make love to me, Storer.'

'Later.'

'Now, Storer, *now*.'

She wasn't naked, but the outfit told him that sex had been on her mind all day. She provoked him, seducing him with her body, tilting her hips and bending her knees to stretch the lace gusset of the panties and make the crinkled satin straps of the suspender bow away from her thighs. The stockings were the colour of pearl, intricately patterned and came up high to the crotch. Two tiny blue bows fastened each side of the panties, another was crushed under the centre of the half-shell bra which supported her breasts and offered them quivering up to his hands. She swayed as she came to him, her body thrown forward by the high heels of the black patent leather shoes. She put her hand out to touch him but he caught her wrist and held it away.

'Cool off, Rena,' he told her.

'You bastard, Storer.'

She let it all go, stalked back to the bed and kicked off her shoes, stripped down the quilt and got in. Furiously she hauled the sheets up round her throat and covered herself. Tossing her blonde hair she bared her teeth at him like a virgin wildly protecting her honour. Storer had never had much time for soft-core pornography even if it was alive and warm. Tonight he had no urge to pander to her. He took the bottle to the wash-stand and made her a drink, half whisky and half tap-water. He carried it back and laid it on the bedside table. She looked at it at first as if it was a tarantula in a gift-wrapped box, then picked it up and comforted herself with it, hugging her knees up to her breasts under the sheet.

Storer sat in the sagging armchair and rubbed his eyes.

'Don't you even want to know what happened?' he asked.

'Yes,' she said meekly. 'Yes, of course I do.'

He told her about Rushton's reaction to the telegram, but left out the bit about Burchill. She said nothing until he had finished, then she put her head on one side and stared at him. She held the glass out, empty. Her hair hung down, and the arm was smooth and white to the crown of the shoulder and the inner curve fed into the hanging breast. She looked more like her sister than ever, Storer thought: or perhaps it was only because he wanted it to be that way. He fetched her another whisky, filling the glass up full with water so that the mixture would last her longer.

'You never told me how you got out of Crumlington without being caught,' Storer said.

'I drove fast.'

'Were you driving?'

'Of course. It was my Ventora.'

'How did you know the case would be in the Merk?'

'He always took it to syndicate meetings.'

'How often do these meetings happen?'

'Once, sometimes twice, each month.'

'Where do they hold them?'

'I don't know,' she said. 'Probably only a couple of dozen people all told know that.'

'Burchill being one of them?'

'Naturally,' she said. 'Burchill is the heir-apparent, the chosen one. When Jack dies, it's Burchill who'll fill his shoes.'

Storer grunted. 'Tomorrow I'll keep looking for you,' he said. 'I'll have to make a lot more smoke before they'll believe I'm working for my money.'

'When will you set it up with my sister?'

'After we've squeezed the lemon a couple of times.'

'Do you know how you're going to do it yet?' Rena asked. 'With the car?'

'With the Ventora,' Storer said, nonchalantly, as if all that part of it was already clear and settled in his mind. 'With your Ventora.'

'Ah, yes.'

'In the meantime,' Storer said, 'We've got to work out the best way to pick up the money.'

'Do you think he'll rig it to try to catch me on the day?'

'Rushton won't,' Storer said, 'but I will.'

Rena giggled; it was too girlish for her and sounded false, part of her bid to please him. She said, 'You're playing against yourself, Storer, both sides of the table at once.'

'Yeah.'

'I wonder who'll win?'

'I will,' Storer said.

She got up on her knees and put the empty glass on the table and let the sheet slip from around her, rocking on the apex of her knees. Her skin was very fair in the soft lamplight. She put one hand under her breast, lifted it and admired it, then looked up at Storer to see if he was admiring it too.

'Is it later yet?' she asked huskily.

Impassively Storer reached for his belt buckle. He was thinking of other things but dripped just enough command into his brain to get the reaction she needed. When he put out the light he was still thinking of other things. Even when he came hard into her he was thinking of Kathy Arden.

5

The first spoonful of soup made her nauseous but she held it down and by the time the bowl was finished she felt better and had begun to think in a straight line again. In the beginning the woman held the bowl for her and guided the spoon to her mouth but latterly she was able to sup it unaided. She drank the tea gladly for she was very thirsty; dope drying out in her system.

The room had changed. She wondered what day it was or whether it was night and if so which night. The junk had all gone; only the solid dresser remained and two chairs and an ancient radio with a hole where the station dial should be. A faint smell of beeswax polish perfumed the air and the bulb had a hideous pink plastic shade over it. Stacked on one chair were half a dozen new magazines and new clothing still in its plastic wrappings – nylons and panties and a woollen twin-set, even a pair of slacks. In an incongruously neat row toilet articles were laid out on the dresser. After Kathy finished her third cup of tea she examined the clothes, silently but without criticism. The woman watched her, silent too.

Kathy said, 'Are you dressing me up for him?'

'In Marks' knickers!' said the woman. 'He wouldn't thank me for that.'

'*Are* you keeping me here for him?' Kathy said. She kept her tone low and calm. 'I mean . . .'

'He's not like that,' the woman said. 'An' if he was I wouldn't be the one t'abet him. Now, it's no good asking me questions because I'm near as much in the dark as you say you are.'

'Can I go to the lavatory?'

'Ay.'

Not until she slipped from the bed did it strike her that escape might be possible. The beginnings of various plots began the slow process of ferilisation. Her legs were weak and her head hurt, but the woman gave her an arm, helped her out of the room and across a darkened landing into the bathroom. The bathroom, like the bedroom, was bare of all but essential furnishings. Kathy surmised that it had been cleaned out for her benefit. The wall-cabinet held the ring marks of medicine or cosmetic bottles, and the mirror on the front of it was still smeared with a film of soap. The bath had brown stains under the taps and the metal plug was rusty. Two towels hung from a nail by the wash-basin. Kathy saw the nail and the chain of the flush as possible weapons now.

As if reading her thoughts the big woman said, 'I wouldn't advise y'to try anything with me, m'dear. I was brought up in a hard school.'

To her embarrassment the woman stood by the door while she made use of the room. She listened for sounds outside to provide a clue as to her whereabouts. The woman was Scottish; Kathy wondered if she had been taken North of the Border. She had never believed the stories in the Sunday newspapers about white slavers, but in spite of her commonsense, she was beginning to have doubts. The window was curtained with a dingy blue material but if it had been day she would have known it. So it was night. One fact was all she had: it was night. She was stuck with the situation; until she worked out how best to use her youth against the big woman's age, she was forced to accept it. Discarding modesty, she stripped off her underwear and washed herself in tepid water. She was shivering long before she was finished, and started when the woman wrapped a bath towel round her shoulders. She was glad to get back into the still-warm bed, dressed in the garish new pyjamas which the woman gave her.

The woman folded her arms, and looked at her sternly, like the matron of a hospital ward.

'Now,' she said, 'you'll have thought about it an' you'll have decided that there's three things you can do. You can try and jump me, knock me out with something heavy, and get downstairs. I should tell you that I'm a very cautious woman with a nut as hard as an iron pot; besides there's folks downstairs wouldn't like it if I got hurt. You *could* try breakin' the lavatory window, only it's boarded up, and anyway it only overlooks the gardens and nobody would hear you if you shouted. Then you could have a go at forcing this door, only you'd have to be very quiet 'cause there's three of us on this landing and we're all light sleepers. Even startin' a fire wouldn't do you much good, maybe you'd choke before we got you out. I'm certain you wouldn't want t'choke.'

'All right,' said Kathy. 'I understand.'

'Maybe,' the woman said, 'you'll think of somethin' else. But my advice t'you, m'dear, is just to rest quiet.' She nodded as if she had finished a set speech, then she said, 'What d'you like special to eat?'

'I'm not hungry.'

'You'll be hungry tomorrow.'

Kathy smiled at her. 'All right,' she said. 'I'll have lamb chops, casseroled not fried. I don't like fried food. Lamb chops and garden peas and whole boiled potatoes.'

'Pudding?'

'Fruit.'

'Breakfast?'

'Cereal, with warm milk please, and coffee. No toast.'

'I never have toast either,' the woman said. 'I lived on toast an' dripping once for near three years; I've never been able to stomach it since.'

'In prison?' Kathy asked.

'You've a cheek, m'lady,' the woman said indignantly. 'I've never been in prison in my life. The very idea.'

Kathy grinned at her again, not because she thought impudence was a form of defence, but because she had gleaned another small fact. She had proved her theory that the woman would talk, trip up now and again and tell her things. If she steered the conversation correctly she could perhaps discover lots of useful information which would later help the police find this house, this woman and that strange commanding man. She thought of that man again. Why was she important to him? She had no doubt that he was behind her abduction. She wondered what he wanted with her. What did he plan to do with her?

'Has he?'

'Who?' the woman said, settling her ruffled feathers.

'The man who brought me here,' Kathy said. 'Has he been in prison?'

'Not him,' the woman replied. Now it was her turn to grin. 'That narrows the field for you, lass. That brings it down to twenty million.'

'Yes,' said Kathy. 'But there's only one like him, isn't there?'

'Isn't there just,' the woman said, throwing back her

head and laughing heartily. 'Och, ay,' she said, 'I can see you an' me'll get along just fine.'

'I hope so,' Kathy said. 'I really hope so.'

Even as the woman laughed Kathy had felt the sweat of fear dew her body again, and tension leap into her limbs. In her throat her own responsive laughter choked; she did not understand the implications of irony which might lie behind the woman's mirth. She was confronted by a wall of her own naïvety. Her life had been spent in and around Manchester. She had lived a safe dull little life as nurse to her ailing mother until the latter had died and, on pure impulse, she had given up her office job and tried to make it as a singer. Her sister had been a singer. She had escaped from Manchester. Rena had gone off like a bird into London, years and years ago, and had presumably found some kind of happiness there, for she never came back: never written or telephoned or called, not even for mother's funeral, though the death had been announced in all the local papers. So she had tried to follow her sister's indistinct path into a life of opportunity and excitement. But she was not like Rena, not in the slightest – except in looks. Rena had always been sharp and wise, brimful of sly confidence in herself and experience of the world. If Rena were here now, she would know what to do. Rena would have some inkling as to what was happening, would know how to handle that man. But Rena was not here. Kathy was alone and her innocence was like lead in her heart.

'Are you sick?' the woman said.

'No.'

'Lie back and sleep again.'

'Yes.'

A moment later the woman went out and locked the door. But Kathy Arden did not sleep. Instead she sat huddled on the bed devising how best she could escape.

6

The effort of resisting a second double whisky exhausted Griggs and he was doubtful if he would make it from the lounge of the Gantry bar to the public call-boxes in back of the cloakroom. He did, just managing to swing out the wooden seat and hitch his buttocks on to it before his legs packed in. He was sweating profusely, sweating and shivering as if he'd had himself a bucketful of booze instead of just one double Scotch. Once he was inside the cubicle with the door closed, however, the world dropped away from him and after a time he felt stronger. Sweat dried and he still had the clean taste of whisky in his mouth. He lit a cigarette, took a huge handful of change from his pocket and spread it on the book rack. There was a tiny square mirror just at eye level; he stared thoughtfully at his face for a moment. Old Henry Griggs – poor old Henry Griggs. Many would be glad to see the last of him drift up in smoke from the crematorium chimney, not that his corpse would make much smoke for all that was left of him. No, his passing would not be mourned – except by Martha and maybe a few fellers like Storer who still found him useful. In a way it was a miracle he had survived so long: he had secrets stored in his head which could put many a shady character in jeopardy of his freedom. He liked to think of himself as a walking encyclopaedia of information. Alex MacAusland had once called him a living library – a phrase which flattered his vanity. The trouble was that so many of the fellers he had taped were either dead or doing bird.

Griggs played with the silver coins, setting them up in little convenient piles. He hoped he had enough pull left, enough favours owing, to find out what Storer was up to. He had never seen Storer so cagey and when a pro like Storer showed it, even in subtle ways, then something wild was in the wind. His curiosity acted like a drug on his jaded system, jagging and reviving him, making his mind clear and sharp again the way it used to be before his cells rioted.

A hundred measly quid! Did Storer imagine that amount was going to make much difference to Martha's welfare? God Almighty, he had knowledge that could net him a hundred times that much – if only he had the guts to turn to blackmail. He had spent a lifetime now learning to sell information, how to barter news and gossip, exchange fact for fact, cross-breed one snippet of chat with another, water and weed and tend isolated rumours until they grew into strong plants – then he sold them. He was not a grasser or a blackmailer though. He bought a few favours now and again, but that was all. Somehow his scruples hadn't done him much good. He was now at the end of the road, living in a council flat and eking out a few miserable savings while others lived fat on the data he'd sold. He could never bring himself to do it for his own sake, but he had Martha's future to think of now. For thirty-eight years she'd stuck by him through thick and thin, mostly thin, and she deserved a better end to her days than he could provide for her. He had no insurance, never thought of it, and no money put away to keep her after he was gone. But Martha never complained; even at this late date she trusted him to provide for her twilight years. She wouldn't have to go back to being a lousy barmaid, or to scrubbing floors, not if he could help it, not now Storer had given him the chance to cash-in on something big. They could put him down if they wanted now: Storer could add his name to his list. It made no bleedin' difference. All that mattered was scraping up a stake for Martha. If he had to cross Storer then he would. God, if he had to cross Rushton he would do that too. Instead of working for one, he would work for both: no harm in that.

Griggs had guessed that Storer was on a double-cross. The whys and wherefores were what he now hoped to unearth. He would not welsh on his deal with Storer: even a hundred quid would be useful. But Rushton had more, much, much more. If his hunch was right then he might have the biggest, juiciest chunk of information he had ever touched, right in the palm of his hand.

He spat the cigarette butt to the floor and ground it out with his heel. Settling himself comfortably for a long evening's work, he dialled the first number and, a moment later, shot home the coin.

'Charlie,' he said. 'Henry here. You remember me, Charlie: Henry Griggs. *That*'s right.' He touched a match to another cigarette. 'Charlie,' he went on, 'you owe me a favour, I think. Well, the time's come to collect.'

7

The roar of the jet aircraft coming in to land drowned out the voices. The men were used to it and stopped speaking, looking towards the window which showed only a blank beige-coloured oblong of sky. They waited patiently for the noise to diminish. Soon it faded off enough for the soundproofing of the hotel suite to hold out what was left. Rushton looked down the table, seeing the slivers of daylight on the carafes and the shine of the window reflected in the polish like a flash of sunlight on the water of a lake. It was difficult for him to read the expression of the man at the head of the table. He could not see the others clearly either and lifted his glasses and pushed them on to his nose. The names of the four men who counted were Browning, Marquand, Mills and Lenihan. They were the syndicate. Seated attentively on the over-stuffed benches which the hotel provided were seven other men, younger than the directors and more tense. Burchill was among them. Rushton knew that Burchill was watching him closely. To Roy he was still the king, but he cherished no illusions as to the exact nature of Burchill's loyalties. In Burchill's book he always came second to the syndicate. The plane passed out of earshot.

When silence settled again, Mills said, 'Pay the lady.'

'But this is only the first bite,' Rushton said. 'She's testing me.'

'Twenty-five thousand isn't lethal, Rushton,' Mills declared. 'I say pay the lady.'

'Get those accounts back,' said Lenihan. 'I don't care how you do it, Rushton, just get them back.'

'I'm trying,' said Rushton.

'We know you are,' Mills said. He had a suave voice like the stroking of a hand over the fur of a Persian cat. 'But as she obviously isn't in it alone, we have a great deal to worry over. We won't be stubborn about it, you know. We're not schoolboys. We know what can happen. The existence of the accounting statements in the wrong hands is a potential threat not only to our immediate security but to most of our future plans. I don't have to draw a diagram, do I?'

'Do you need men?' Browning asked.

Rushton shook his head. 'Information.'

'Don't you realise how serious this is?' Marquand said with sudden vehemence.

'Calm,' Mills said. 'Calm. We're not immediately threatened.'

'I say we are,' Lenihan declared. 'I say we are and I say cut him out now.'

'Hold on,' Rushton said. 'You forget who I am.'

He glanced over at Burchill. Burchill's tongue was on his nether lip and he might have been smiling. On occasions Rushton hated the young man whom he had picked as his successor, not only hated but feared him. Burchill was like a prowling tiger, and as of this minute Rushton felt about as secure as a tethered goat.

'Anyhow, Lenihan,' he went on, 'it's too tightly knit to cut me off just like that. If you imagine I'm just going to let you sell me out because some stupid bitch . . .'

'Your lady wife,' Lenihan said. 'Let's not forget that, Rushton. *Your* lady wife.'

'Listen,' said Rushton angrily, 'I was the founder of this organisation. I selected you – all of you – one by one. My brain and my capital, my contacts opened up almost every . . .'

'Don't give me all that ancient history crap,' Lenihan said.

'We're not brawling in Benny's back room now, gentlemen,' Mills said. 'We're no longer dependent on . . . the old methods, if you take my meaning. It's not the first mistake one of us has made. One thing is clear, however, you *must* pay the first demand. Of course, you'll keep us informed of every development: in turn we'll endeavour to discover where your wife is and who's working with her.'

'They can really hit us big,' said Lenihan. 'They knew what they were doing when they picked those accounts. The gold ship . . .'

'Lenihan,' Mills said. 'It's a rats' nest in the basement. If we can't smoke out a rats' nest then we don't deserve to be in control, do we?'

'Yer,' said Lenihan, 'you're right. What's the drill?'

'Simple really,' said Mills. 'Let Rushton pay the first bill, out of his own pocket of course, then we must all assist in finding Rena. I suppose, Rushton, you wouldn't count that as interference?'

Rushton shook his head.

'But if we don't find her?' Browning said. 'Aren't we all in trouble?'

'We'll find her,' said Mills. 'Somebody's bound to know where she is and who she's with, and that somebody will tell us.'

'Why should they?' asked Lenihan.

'Because,' said Mills patiently, 'we can afford to pay more than anyone else for the information.'

'Yer,' said Rushton. 'It's true. I've got somebody on it already.'

'Storer?' Marquand asked.

'That's right,' said Rushton surprised. 'How did you know?'

'If my wife ran off with my future in her pocket,' Marquand said, 'I'd hire Storer too.'

'Have her . . . removed, by all means,' Mills said. 'That's your privilege. But not until we find the nest. Is that clear, Rushton, *not until we find the nest.*'

8

Ma MacAusland hummed a highland air to herself as she stirred the creamy porridge in the black iron pot. The pot and the wooden spurtle were reminders of her youth in Glasgow. She always thought of Alex when she used the stirring spurtle, but she used it seldom now. She herself could not stand porridge and could not understand how the girl could ask for it specially. Maybe the lass was trying to curry favour with her. Ma shook her head at the thought and murmured to herself, 'Och, no, she's not like that.'

In recent years she had fallen into the habit of talking to herself, holding fragmentary conversations as she went about her multitude of minor chores. Laziness was not her natural vice but just a kind of aimlessness, a belief that what didn't get done today would get done tomorrow. Her attitude had all but driven Alex mad. He had been a really fussy bugger when he was young but he had yielded to her ways rather than she to his. She was always stronger than him. Perhaps, if she had been more ambitious she could have driven him on to greater things, but the four years in the Scrubs put paid to that. After that stretch he was scared of the big stuff and would not co-operate with anyone. She had Frank to keep her company; Frank never seemed to mind what state she kept the house in. In some ways Frank was dearer to her than her husband. She was devoted to her foster son, though she let little enough of the devotion show through. She made no demands of him; fed him, washed his clothes, saw to his education and did not indulge in the hypocrisy of trying to stop Alex making a crook out of him. Whatever he did for his money, Frank Storer was a good boy and had never shirked his responsibility to her. Still, she got lonely sometimes, and sometimes wished that it had all been different. If only Frank had brought the girl back openly.

'He never could,' she told the pimply face of the porridge. 'He couldn't have a girl like her in a hundred years.'

She liked the girl. Even with a careful guard on her tongue she enjoyed talking to her. She knew what the minx was up to all right, trying to wheedle information out of her about Frank and all the rest of it; but she could be crafty too and had fed the lass enough nonsense mixed with the truth to keep her permanently puzzled. Ma tried not to think of what Storer and that other hussy, the sister, wanted with Kathy. She did not take to the sister at all and, under Storer's specific instructions, had never mentioned her to the girl upstairs. It was nice to have somebody in the house.

'A captive audience,' she said to herself and chuckled. 'Ay, a real captive audience.'

She filled a soup plate with thick porridge, stood a

cream jug and sugar bowl beside it and loaded the lot on to a tray. Carefully she carried the tray upstairs, then, supporting it in one hand, took the key from her apron pocket and unlocked the door. She turned the handle and went in. The light was out and it was dark in the room. In the faint glow from the bathroom she could see the shape of the girl huddled under the clothes. Sleeping her head off again – the lazy thing. With the tray balanced on her left hand Ma shuffled forward. She reached for the switch on the right wall. As the light came on, the base of the drawer from the top of the dresser struck her on the back of the head.

It did not strike her cleanly but glanced off just above her ear. The spine-like growth of curlers absorbed much of the force of the blow and Ma did not lose consciousness even for a moment. She staggered though, ducking, so that the flat of the drawer hit her next across the shoulders, hurting her. The tray was already falling and she swung it round and flung it hard, hearing the girl yelp and her own groans and the crash of crockery as it tumbled to the floor. The girl was wiping porridge from her eyes; her arms were coated with a gritty mixture of fresh milk and sugar. She shook her head like a heifer.

Ma chopped her briskly on the muscle of the upper arm and the drawer thudded down among the mess on the carpet. Ma stepped forward, braced herself, and swung up her right fist. It connected with the point of the girl's chin. The girl reeled back, then swayed. Ma caught her as she pitched forward again. She threw her on the bed and, breathing heavily, picked her way carefully over the spilled porridge and broken plates out on to the landing.

She locked the door and went into the bathroom. A sticky trail of oatmeal footprints chased her up to the lavatory. She sat down and, reaching to the basin beside her, ran the cold tap. She put her head against the edge of the basin and gathered her breath. There was a tiny fleck of blood on her scalp where one of the curlers had pricked her, but her head hardly hurt at all. Her back was painful though: she tried to reach round to rub it, but found that she was too fat. She washed her face in freezing water and bathed her wound, such as it was, then went downstairs to make tea for herself and coffee for the girl.

There was no malice in Ma, no anger that Kathy had tried to escape. In fact she was almost pleased: it would get it out of her system. She grunted with the ache across her back: all that bruised flesh. And all that mess to clean up in the bedroom. When the minx came round and recovered sufficiently she could clean it up herself – under supervision. Ma did not feel like bending at the moment.

The kettle hissed and bubbled. She spooned Nescafé into a cup and added boiling water. As she stirred up the fragrant brown liquid she ruefully considered her earlier judgement and revised it now, volubly.

'She's spunky enough,' Ma said. 'Maybe she would do for him after all.'

The thought pleased her. She chuckled, then laughed at her own romantic naïvety. Nature never made a pair yet out of such diverse material. Then suddenly she stopped laughing and not only because it hurt her back. She wished Frank had kept her out of it. She was becoming too involved. It wasn't because of Kathy's attack that she was afraid. What Ma feared was her undiminished fondness for the lass.

She took the cup of fresh hot coffee and poured it quickly down the sink. Then in a fit of violent pique flung the cup itself hard up against the wall.

'More mess,' she shouted, as fragments exploded all over the kitchen. 'More bloody mess.'

9

At eleven-thirty on Wednesday morning in the private bedroom above the deserted tables of the Stag's Palace, Rushton woke. The faint drone of a vacuum cleaner penetrated the walls of the room, but Rushton could not distinguish between that familiar morning sound and the buzzing of the sexual hangover locked in his head. Even the distant rumble of a truck below the curtained windows he interpreted as a protest of his system to the beating it had taken the night before. Burchill's suggestion that a session with the right kind of girl would cure his fit of black dog had seemed like a good idea at the time. The girl was still beside him: he could feel the warmth of her flanks against his thighs. She was a Jamaican and her skin was the colour of tarnished gold, rich with a youthful suppleness at which Rushton could only marvel.

Burchill had chosen the girl well; she liked all the things that Rushton did to her but did not exceed her brief by demanding more than he was capable of giving. She suffered her frustration and the heat of her body in dewy silence, groaning when he pinched her firm bottom or clamped his hands on her small-nippled breasts. He had a geyser of anger in him which made him cruel: yet Burchill had been astute enough to fetch him a girl so unlike Rena that he could perform his trivial outrages on her without any memories spiking his guns or spoiling his sadistic pleasure. He could never be cruel to Rena: he might start off to hurt her, but he could never follow through with it. Conditioned reflex had caused his impotence to extend to all big-breasted blondes. But the Jamaican had been just what he needed – last night. This morning what he needed was a bath-chair and a tartan rug. Sixty was a dangerous age for a man to lose control of himself and he had gone on and on with the girl, anxious to prove himself to her, to get more reaction from her than the whining and crying of pain. Eventually he had succeeded and had rooted from her a shrill howl of gratification and relief before he let her go and, rolling over like an old lion, had fallen instantly asleep.

With only a few hours' undisturbed slumber since Rena left, he felt closer to death than life. His brain fumbled over the duties of the day. To comfort himself he turned his face into the girl's coarse black hair and inhaled the peculiar exciting odour of it. The loamy fragrance reminded him of a paddock just after rain. On mornings like this one he sometimes yearned for the simplicity of his early career on the course. He had only to obey orders then and not bear responsibility for them. The girl stirred and nuzzled against him: he appreciated the gesture. He stroked her lightly with his cupped palm the way he used to stroke his favourite horse just before a race. His headache eased off and he dropped into a doze tinged with pleasant dreams of race-tracks and youth.

Light drenched him like a sheet of icy water. Cursing, he sat up.

'Sorry,' Burchill said.

Rushton cursed him some more. He hated Burchill for his coolness, handsomeness and youth. Inscrutably, Burchill waited until the boss had finished insulting him. A dark-skinned arm emerged from beneath the clothes. The narrow pink palm showed as the fingers opened and clutched lazily at full consciousness. Rushton snapped at the girl, ordering her to be still.

'What the hell is it, Roy?' Rushton asked. 'And close that damn' curtain, will you.'

Burchill stepped forward and laid the telegram in the hollow of Rushton's knees, then obediently moved to close the curtains and cut off the frosty noonday light.

Rushton slipped his spectacles from the stagskin case on the bedside table and, scowling, read the printed message.

The telegram said: TWENTY-FIVE IN LOW DENOMINATIONS UNMARKED STOP CONVENIENT PARCEL STOP YOU PERSONALLY AND ALONE STOP BRITISH MUSEUM TEN-THIRTY THURSDAY MORN STOP CONTACT WILL BE MADE STOP PRICE OF INITIAL STORAGE ONLY STOP GOODS WILL BE RETAINED STOP PURCHASE PRICE A QUARTER MILLION STOP SILENCE IS GOLDEN STOP LOVE RENA STOP.

Rushton groaned and got out of bed.

'We should be able to pick up the collector at the British Museum,' Burchill said. 'We can cover the place.'

'Me personally,' Rushton said. 'Me.'

'Will I have the money ready, or do you want me to set up a dummy?'

'God, no,' said Rushton quickly. He kneaded his

brow with a stubby finger and thumb. 'It better be the real thing. I don't want to call her bluff just yet.'

'You won't be in any personal danger,' Burchill assured him. 'I'll organise it, shall I?'

'Organise it so we trap him, whoever it is.'

'You don't anticipate that your . . . wife will make the pick-up herself?'

'Never,' said Rushton. 'She's not that crazy.'

'Shall I tell Storer?' asked Burchill. 'He'll probably call in some time today. He knows the instructions are due.'

'Tell Storer and tell Mills too,' said Rushton. 'I want half a dozen men – the best – on the scene when I go in.'

'Planted in the museum,' said Burchill. 'Presumably not looking like dicks or out-of-work wrestlers.'

'Yer,' said Rushton.

He handed the telegram to Burchill and glanced over his shoulder at the bed. His headache was back. He wanted to be alert and fit for tomorrow. He thought he would sleep for a while longer then go round to the Health Club for a session of steam and massage. The Jamaican was still huddled under the clothes, lying doggo. Rushton poked the hump with his fist.

'Get up, little girl,' he said. 'You can go now.'

He nodded to Burchill who nodded back in sign that appropriate payment would be made.

'Again tonight?' Burchill asked.

'No,' said Rushton. He would need all his wits about him tomorrow morning.

The men watched as the naked girl disentangled herself from the bed clothes then, without the least trace of modesty, strolled into the bathroom. Her firm high-riding buttocks moved like oil and for some reason her nipples were still erect, like two nicotine-stained fingertips standing up from the small breasts. Rushton hitched up his pyjama pants.

'She was good, Roy,' he said. 'You did well.'

'Thank you,' Burchill said. Roy was always very polite.

Rushton shook off his lethargy, went into the lounge and seated himself behind his desk. He lifted the telephone, ordered breakfast, and pretended to read *The Times.* The flutter of nervousness was in his stomach again and he looked down at the ugly folds of white skin, almost expecting to see them visibly throb and writhe. He had no way of combating fear. It would mount gradually until this business was over. Fear was always part of it, but in the last ten years he had grown so accustomed to security that he had all but forgotten the sensation. Even now his heart was thumping in his chest like a prisoner beating on a dungeon wall. He was too old to be persecuted in this way. If only Storer would come up with something immediately he might not have to go through the hell of delivering the money himself. The British Museum: why in God's name pick such a place? Rena probably thought she was being funny. He listened to the creep of apprehension in his gut, then shivered.

'Roy,' he shouted. 'Bring me my robe.'

He waited, looking up expectantly at the bedroom door.

'Roy.'

He got up and went into the bedroom and shouted again, 'Roy?' But Burchill had gone.

10

Working with Burchill, Storer set up the distribution of men borrowed from the syndicate. There were six of them, plus Burchill, plus Storer, plus Rushton. Storer knew what the telegram meant: it meant Rushton had to enter the Museum and walk the long central aisle under the enigmatic guard of great stone statues, past the raised, glazed stalk of the Rosetta Stone, climb the open staircase at the back of the building and quarter the rooms on the second floor. Rena, it seemed, had no intention of being funny. Early morning before the drop, Storer briefed the men and arranged them in a shifting screen so that Rushton, left to pick his own route, would never be out of someone's reach for a minute. The heavies were equipped with notebooks and eyeglasses and told to impersonate sightseers: only a couple of them were ever likely to succeed.

Nervous as a cat, Rushton could not understand why the telegram had been so vague. Storer, with the authority of a man who can admire an enemy's guile, explained that fluidity of the arrangement made a stake-out difficult. Whoever was working with Rena, Storer said, knew what he was doing. In addition to the trailers in the building Storer placed six more of Rushton's mob in three cars strategically situated at Montague Street, Russell Square and Bloomsbury Street. They were in position by eight-thirty, two full hours before the drop. The men in the building, including two on the front steps, were ready by ten-five.

It was a fine sharp morning, clear as glass. The edifices of London town, gilded by the sun, were fixed solidly against a translucent blue sky. Early morning frost melted quickly on the sunshine side leaving the roads striped white and damp black. Burchill and Storer sat in the front, Burchill driving, while Rushton pressed himself against the stout upholstery of the Mercedes as if a great wall of acceleration was building up on him. The car crawled out of Soho.

'How do you know it's not a plot to rub me out?' Rushton asked plaintively.

'She wants you alive,' Storer said. 'If she'd only wanted you dead she would have found a simpler way to do it.'

'But why me, in person? I don't understand it,' Rushton whined.

'Joke,' Burchill said softly.

'Some joke,' said Rushton. 'It's terrible.'

'You've nothing to worry about,' Storer said. 'We've covered all the angles.'

The Merk nosed its way across Oxford Street into Tottenham Court Road. Burchill set it up to make the turn into Great Russell Street: then it happened. The Mini came abreast of them and swivelled on its attenuated axis to block the left nearside wing of the Merk.

'Dammit,' Burchill said, and looked behind him. When he glanced left again Rena Rushton's face filled the open space of the window close to Storer's and the snub nose of the revolver, shielded by a large white handbag, was pointed into the interior of the car. Burchill jerked and slid his hand towards the switch for the automatic window device.

'No,' Rena said. 'Don't touch it.'

Rushton was staring at her as if she was the ghost of one of his past victims.

'Touch anything, Roy, or you Storer, and your boss is dead.'

'Please, Rena,' Rushton whispered, 'don't kill me.'

Storer could see his head in the mirror. He did not turn round. Rushton's skin was shiny with a sudden sweat which ran over the drained flesh like perspiration on a lump of gelignite: only Rushton wasn't going to explode.

'The key, Roy,' Rena said.

'What?'

'Give me the key.'

Storer reached out and took the key and offered it in his palm. He was sweating too. Rena picked it up and held it in her left hand, keeping the arrangement of handbag and revolver back from the window. Behind the Mercedes a few cars were lined up, honking impatiently. Storer was watching them too as best he could, watching them and Rushton and Burchill and the woman.

'Now the parcel,' she said.

The parcel, wrapped in brown paper and tied with string, sat on Rushton's knee. He handed it to Storer, but Rena said, 'You, Jack, you put it through the window: lean over and do it.'

Rushton did. Storer moved his shoulders. The woman had thought it all out well; she was able to hook the string of the parcel in her left hand without losing the focus of the gun muzzle on Rushton's face even for an instant. Storer hoped that Burchill was drinking in the cleverness of it all.

'Put up the window, Roy,' she said. 'The right switch.'

Burchill did it: the three men watched the glass slide up. She was still there and the gun was still there but with the windows closed they seemed cut off from her. Storer could see her smiling as she turned the key in the lock and imprisoned them completely. Then she was gone: not into the Mini again, but on foot, walking quickly away. Rushton craned his neck to watch her. She wore an expensive suit of a demure pink colour which showed off her figure, her hips swinging with a kind of sexual insolence and her blonde hair, let down, bobbed out its soft ends from under the headband. She held the handbag in one hand and the parcel in the other.

'God,' Rushton moaned. 'God, she did it.'

Rena vanished round the corner into Oxford Street.

Burchill was already on the radio to the other cars, but before they arrived quite a crowd of curious and irate drivers were clustered round the Mercedes and its three prisoners. Some shook their fists and gesticulated, others laughed. In the back of the car, Rushton bent forward with his head in his hands like a man in prayer. Still growling into the hand-mike, Burchill kept his eyes on the floor, but Storer stared back at them through the windscreen, having a hard time not to grin with the secret pleasure of a job well done.

11

By one-thirty the post mortem had fizzled out and Rushton was well on his way to being stoned. From time to time the phone rang and a disconsolate male voice asked for further instructions. Burchill would cup his hand over the receiver and pass the message on to the boss, and the boss would lift his head from his chest, raise one elbow from the desk top, wave the glass and say harshly, 'Keep looking, keep looking.' Burchill would sigh and cock his shoulder and repeat the message into the telephone wearily.

Storer was surprised that nobody blamed him for the foul-up. Rushton, too miserable to think reasonably, had elevated his wife to the status of a criminal mastermind, thereby absolving a mere professional like Storer from culpability. On the other hand, Burchill's casual acceptance of the mess worried Storer; he would have been better pleased if the aide had blistered him for his carelessness and lack of foresight. Burchill even seemed to think that commiseration was in order and had apologised meekly to Storer, consoling him with the reassurance that he too thought the stake-out adequate.

Storer managed to eat a considerable lunch: the events of the morning had not upset Burchill's appetite either. Neither of them touched liquor though and the meal was punctuated by phone-calls from the searchers. Storer was confident that the syndicate's boys would not pick up Rena's trail. By this time she would be safe back in the Gresham counting the haul. He wished that he could be with her now: not to make love to her or even share her moment of triumph, just to keep an eye on her.

Rushton filled his glass again and thumped the bottle on the leather of the desk. The bottle was empty. He did not lip the glass until the dead man had been removed and a fresh bottle of whisky, with the cork loosened, had taken its place. Then he drank, slowly but deeply, and belched into his closed fist. His face was ruddy with the heat of the liquor and his eyes were pouched in discoloured fat.

He said, 'What do we do now, Storer?'

Storer said, 'Wait for the next telegram.'

'Clever bitch,' Rushton said. 'She knows I'm a sitting duck.'

'Yeah,' said Storer. 'I'm afraid you are.'

'I could crush an outsider,' Rushton said, 'but she knows how my mind works. I never told her a thing either. I mean, I kept business and pleasure strictly separate. I wouldn't want anybody t'think I'd told her all my . . .'

The telephone rang again. Burchill lifted it, nodded. He held it out to Rushton, 'Mr Marquand.'

'Oh, Jesus!' Rushton said. He finished the whisky, looking over the rim bug-eyed at the offered receiver. When he took the glass away and reached for the instrument his eyes were hard and angry.

'Marquand. She got off with it. She did it alone.'

The voice on the other end of the wire said something prolonged. Rushton sighed, then waved his hand at the two men in the room. Burchill got up and went to the door; Storer followed him. Just before Burchill closed the door Storer heard Rushton shouting into the phone: 'Of course she was bloody clever. Of course it wasn't his fault.'

In a little while, Storer decided, he would be able to make a prudent departure. With stage one successfully completed Rena would be anxious to plan the strategy for stage two. Then he had his own deal cooking: Griggs might have information for him by now. And he must check with Ma MacAusland that all was well in Watford.

The Stag's Palace was dark and empty. Behind the bar a young man in a white jacket was assiduously polishing the counter with fluid from an aerosole canister. In spilled light through the archways Storer saw shrouded tables and gilt-backed chairs like props in a melodrama waiting for the actors to possess them and give them weight and meaning. In the back room someone was tuning the Steinway and little staccato piles of notes spilled out of the darkness like copper coins running on their rims down an oaken board. It was a sad sound which, after a minute or two, played on the nerves as well as on the emotions. The main foyer was silent and, when Burchill closed the baffle door, the piano's notes cut off abruptly.

'I'd better not waste any time,' Storer said.

'You're not going on the wild-goose chase too,' Burchill said. It was a statement, not a question. Storer put his hands in his trouser pockets and fingered the keys of the Porsche.

'I don't want to be around when the syndicate get here,' Storer said.

'You have no reason to be afraid of them,' Burchill said. 'Have you?'

'I'm not afraid of them,' Storer said. 'I just think they might blame me for muffing the job.'

'They've all made mistakes in their time,' Burchill said. 'I'm sure they'll understand.'

'Anyway,' Storer said, moving towards the locked front door of the building, 'I have a couple of leads I want to check out.'

'In that case,' Burchill said, 'I won't keep you.'

He took a key-ring from his pocket and slipped one key into the hole low on the padded surface of the door. Burchill did not open the door at once, however, but stood with his hand against it, watching Storer intently. Storer stared back: his stomach muscles tensed almost as if intuition told him that Burchill was going to hit him.

Burchill did not hit him. Burchill said, 'Have you met Rena Rushton before, Storer?'

'Nope,' Storer said.

'Then how come she recognised you?'

'Did she?'

'She called you Storer.'

'I've never seen her before that I know of,' Storer said. 'Perhaps . . .'

'Perhaps what, Storer?'

'Nothing,' Storer said. 'Just a passing thought.'

'It's certainly worth thinking about,' Burchill said. 'Isn't it?'

'Yeah,' Storer agreed. 'It's odd.'

'Let me know if you come up with an answer,' Burchill said.

'Sure,' Storer said. 'I'll let you know.'

He was going to have to keep an eye on Burchill, a very close eye indeed. The boy was sharp; too sharp for his own or anybody else's definite good. Storer turned the corner into Denmark Street and paused in a doorway to light a cigarette. Nobody came round the corner. That didn't mean he had no tail: it just meant that nobody came round the corner. It was a fine afternoon, though cold: just the right kind of afternoon, Storer decided, to take himself for a long, long walk. He struck right for Oxford Street and its maze of department stores. If he had a tail he would lose him there. He could pick up the Porsche later. Right now it was important that he got back to Rena Rushton.

12

She admitted him reluctantly only after he had rapped on the door with increasing impatience for several minutes. The parcel was open on the bed, more than half empty. The notes on the bedside table fluttered in the draught from the opening door. One fiver drifted up and winged to the carpet under the bed as if it was trying to hide from him. The revolver and the head-scarf were on the chair. It was cold in the room and the first thing Storer did was feed shillings into the electric heater; then he came over to the bed where Rena was. Her lips moved to the rhythm of her counting and she had a sheet of Gresham stationery and her ball-point ready to hand, figures on it in columns.

'It's all there,' Storer said. 'All twenty-five thousand of it.'

'I'd just as soon count it, if you don't mind.'

'I can't see why you're all excited about a mere twenty-five,' Storer said. 'You walked out on more than that.'

Rena made another mark on the paper and tucked the pen behind her ear. She looked up at him. 'Did I do it well, Storer?'

Storer grinned. 'Perfect.'

'Are you in trouble?'

'Nope,' said Storer. 'Not with Rushton anyway.'

'Burchill?'

Storer hesitated. 'No.'

She laid her hand flat on the money. 'This is only the beginning, Storer. Next time we'll hit him for the whole bundle.'

'I'm worried about the syndicate,' Storer said. 'Rushton can't pick up a quarter of a million just by snapping his fingers. Some of it, most of it, will be syndicate money.'

'They'll pay,' Rena said.

Storer lowered himself to the bed beside her and lifted a fiver from the parcel. He felt it between finger and thumb the way a corn-merchant might test the quality of grain. 'I'll take my whack now.'

'You're not thinking of backing out?' Rena said.

'No.'

'I suppose ten thousand's a lot to you?'

'It's a lot to most people,' Storer said. 'Even to your beloved husband.'

'But stacked alongside a quarter of a million . . .'

'He won't part with that amount so easily, Rena.'

'I know it.'

'You'll be draining the syndicate,' Storer said. 'It won't be a personal matter between you and Rushton any more. Right about now you'll have Mills and Marquand, Lenihan and Browning all beginning to fret about how far you really will go.'

'All the way.'

'Nothing less?'

'Nothing less,' she said.

'Where's the case, Rena?'

'I'm not telling.'

'I could make you tell.'

'Threats now, is it?' She shook her head. 'Storer, I'd die first.'

'Maybe,' Storer said. 'Anyway, it doesn't matter. So long as it's in safe keeping.'

'It is,' she said.

'I'll take my ten now all the same,' Storer said.

'Cagey,' she said. 'Are you going to give it to that woman?'

'What woman?' Storer asked.

'Your mother?'

'You're joking,' Storer said. 'She wouldn't know what to do with ten thousand quid.'

'Perhaps you underestimate her,' Rena said. She moved the pen from her ear and pointed with it at the larger bundle on the table-top. 'There's ten there, Storer, all nicely counted out for you. Just remember, there's lots more where that came from.'

She chewed the end of the ball-point. It left a tiny blot of blue ink on her lip. 'We've shown him we mean business,' she said. 'Next week we'll organise the sale. No sense in peeling it off him piece by piece. It only adds to the risk.'

'Are you going to do it all alone?' Storer said indulgently.

'How can I?' Rena said. 'I need your help, Storer. If I didn't need your help you wouldn't be here right now, would you?'

'What's the drill?'

'Thursday today,' she said. 'Tomorrow we send him the bill of sale, telling him that the return of the brief-case will cost him a quarter of a million pounds.'

'Rena, do you realise the bulk of two hundred and fifty thousand pounds?'

'I've thought of that,' she said briskly. 'I'll take fifty thousand in notes and the remainder in diamonds.'

'Diamonds?'

'Quality cut stones,' she said. 'Marquand's the diamond expert. He can lay hands on two hundred thousand pounds worth without much trouble. He can put the syndicate in hock for them if he has to. I think they've a good enough case for credit.'

'Diamonds,' said Storer again. 'It might take months

to realise the money in stones. How do I get my cut?'

'You'll be paid in stones,' Rena said.

'I'm no judge of ice,' Storer said.

'Nor am I, but I have a contact in Paris who'll convert into dollars and filter the money into Europe for us.'

'How do we get the diamonds out of the country?' Storer said. 'Tote them in your handbag?'

'They don't have to go out of the country,' Rena said. 'We'll make the sale here.'

'You really have been busy,' Storer said.

'The pick-up will be the trickiest part,' she said. 'I see it like this: we send the demand with instructions that you and Burchill . . .'

'Burchill?'

'Any two men then,' Rena said irritated at being interrupted, 'so long as you're one of them.'

'They won't trust me that far,' said Storer. 'I'm only an outsider in this caper remember. I've bungled once already, and . . .'

'Shut up, Storer,' Rena said. She tapped the pen against the front of his shirt as if it was a stiletto and she was buying his attention with fear. 'They *will* trust you because the day before the pick-up you'll deliver my corpse: only it won't be my corpse.'

'Kathy?'

'Exactly,' the woman said. 'That's your part of it. Set it up so that the "accident" is witnessed by Burchill, or somebody reliable. Give them the body of Rena Rushton, then, just as old Daddy is beginning to relax, we hit him with another telegram telling him that the deal is still on. He'll trust you enough then to let you go. Is that understood?'

'It might work.'

'Take collection in a lonely place, you and Burchill.'

'Where do you come in?'

'I don't,' she said.

'Then who brings the briefcase?'

'Nobody brings the briefcase,' she said. 'I'll have the briefcase.'

'Yeah,' Storer said slowly. 'Sure: I get it. I plan a road-block round the point of exchange, only we never get to the point of exchange. Only Burchill and I are alone in the car, then I can take him and put him out of the game and lift the money and diamonds and *really* lay my head on the block. With you supposedly dead, I draw them off. I become target number one. Jesus, you've cooked up a nice number for me, haven't you?'

'A quarter of a million, Storer,' she said. 'And the whole world's your oyster.'

'It might not be big enough,' Storer said.

'It'll take them an hour at least to find out what the hell's going on,' Rena said. 'Maybe longer. By that time you'll be on the night-flight to Glasgow. Back home, Storer: is that right?'

'Supposing there's fog?'

Rena shrugged. 'Hole out in London.'

'With the loot?' said Storer. 'You wouldn't trust me that far.'

'You'll have the loot,' Rena said, 'but I'll have the contact.'

'In Glasgow?'

'Of course.'

'They'll track us down, Rena,' Storer said. 'The syndicate's a big organisation.'

'They're not the law,' Rena said. 'They can't cover the entire country, Storer. Even if you've to travel by road, you can make it north. We exchange the diamonds for bank serials and clear out to Europe any time we like.'

'And the fifty thousand?'

'You get fifteen in hand.'

'And the rest?'

'I have to pay off a few people.'

'I don't like it, Rena,' Storer said. 'I don't like any of it.'

'Because you'll be the pigeon?'

'That among other things.'

'What other things?'

'Too many other things,' said Storer. 'It's shot through with possibilities for failure.'

'No more than any other big scheme,' Rena said. 'The trouble with you, Storer, is that you lack imagination. Maybe you are a number one boy with a gun, but how long would it take you to earn fifty thousand by rubbing out little men on the fringe of the organisation? A lifetime, Storer, and every time you take on a job it's a risk.'

'I calculate the risks,' said Storer. 'I run the odds.'

'You're in too deep, Storer,' she said. 'You've got to go through with it.'

'I can still take my ten thousand and vanish,' Storer said.

'But you won't, Storer.'

'No,' he said, after a while, 'I won't.'

'Good boy,' she said. 'Admit I'm clever.'

'You're clever all right,' Storer said.

'I've a surfeit of imagination,' she said. 'That's my

trouble. Did you really think *all* I had on my mind was sex?'

'Haven't you?'

'I have now,' she said. 'I've done my little chores for today, Storer. Now I want my fun, some imaginative fun. I've lots of tricks up my sleeve, not just my sleeve. Like to see them?'

She took off the top of the suit and she was naked underneath. She flung it across the room. The draught pulled a few more fivers after it.

'Come on, Storer,' she said huskily. 'No risk involved.'

She was as high as a kite on the excitement and triumph of the morning and, though he felt only nagging anxiety and the fretful urgency of a man for whom time is running out, he did what she wanted. He was abrupt and violent with her, pounding her until she cried out. Soon after the start, the parcel of money slid down the pillow and the notes spread out under them, crisp and brittle like a carpet of bleached leaves.

When it was over he rose from her at once, gathered his share of the money from the table and stuffed it into the pockets of his jacket. She was still lying on the carpet of crumpled bank-notes, her naked limbs fair against the bruised paper background, her eyes closed and her mouth open, sated for once with what he had done to her. Storer switched out the lamp and, with the heavy jacket draped over his arm, gladly left the room.

He knew now that she planned to double-cross him but that Rena too was only a tool, an instrument of someone sharp and cunning and well-connected, a real professional. He even thought he knew who it might be. Somehow he would have to find out, before he outlived his usefulness and wound up another dead decoy, like Kathy Arden. Tomorrow he would go call on Henry Griggs.

Part Three

1

Friday's morning sun retained the glacial brightness of Thursday but low on the western horizon cloud now lay like tar-paper frieze. Storer drove the Porsche over Chelsea Bridge. The river ran dark as mid-winter night; even the rush of the ebb tide cut no warm shades across its surface. The towers of the power station were sugar pink against the sky but their shadows cleft the park like daggers of chipped flint. Even with the heater blowing warm air across him Storer shivered and pulled the sheepskin coat tighter around him. He wondered if Griggs would be out of bed yet.

Lambeth was a place of red and gold patched with unmelted icing-white frost in parks and playing-fields and postcard gardens. The women who came and went about the approaches of the high flats were huddled in bulky coats and bound with woollen headscarves. Thick-gloved fists clutched the handles of empty shopping bags. A delivery boy, trim as an icicle in his grocer's overall, blew on his hands and hoisted the basket up on his elbow. Babies snug in blankets in their prams had ruddy cheeks and little drips at the tips of their unformed noses.

Storer stuck his hands in the tattered pockets of the coat and ran across the pathway to the block. It was colder inside than out. The corridors held a pearly haze around their neon lamps and the atmosphere was hoary-still like the air in an ice-house. In his anxiety to get out of the cold Storer rapped on Griggs's door as imperiously as a young copper. He gave Griggs a couple of minutes to get himself out of bed, then knocked again. No answer. Storer glanced down the narrow corridor but it was empty. Two pints of milk stood by the side of the flat door. He put his ear against the flimsy woodwork but heard no sound. From his pocket he removed a pair of black-leather driving gloves and put them on. Stooping, he lifted the letter-box lid and peered through the slot into the hall. He frowned, and let the lid down quietly. Stepping back he braced himself against the opposite wall and cocked his right knee up to the level of his belly. Pushing off with his hands he straightened his leg and smashed his heel against the door panel above the lock. It cracked. He backed off and repeated the performance. Though the lock itself held firm, the hollow panel and its scant trimming rent apart. The chain, he noticed, was not in place and the door hung open. Storer stepped inside and closed up the broken door as best he could. He went down on one knee beside the woman's body. She had been dead for some time.

Storer closed his eyes at the sight. The condition of her head reminded him of the Negro he had once beaten to death, and the memory touched the only duct of squeamishness in him. Aimed at the forehead, the force of the blow had smashed the front of her skull, driving shards of bone down into the eye sockets. Falling towards the door of the kitchenette she had also been struck three or four times across the back of the head: brain matter matted with the jelly of blood on her hair. She was still dressed in her overcoat. Her lisle stockings were wrinkled and loose on her thighs and the knitted gloves looked empty on her hands. The shopper was hooked to her right hand. Cans and packets spilled from it: three eggs, cracked and leaking like tiny skulls, had rolled across the lino. Martha Griggs was never a big woman, but in death she seemed to have shrivelled up like a chrysalis from which the butterfly had struggled free. Storer stepped over the body into the living-room.

In contrast Henry Griggs had died passively; with a rictus drawing the flesh, he appeared to be smiling. His eyes were wide open. They were no longer dusty or boozy red but had a dull gloss to them like clay pellets. He was seated in his armchair, head back as if caught in the rapture of faint sweet music. There were no visible marks on him.

Working now with automatic briskness Storer opened the front of the dead man's jacket and felt the pocket: it was empty. He explored the other pockets, moving the corpse firmly and without revulsion. Anger was the insulation he used at times like this and it did not fail him now. All Griggs's pockets were empty. Storer settled the body in the position in which he had found it, and scanned the room. It gave no sign of having been searched. Though the curtains were drawn over the windows none of the lights was lit. Storer tried the lamp switch and found that the bulb had burned out. He returned to the hall and looked in the shopping bag and pulled out the folded newspaper: yesterday's *Evening News*, mid-afternoon edition. Safe to assume that the Griggs, husband and wife, had been put down late Thursday afternoon or early evening.

Storer searched the other rooms quickly, but found nothing to add to his meagre collection of facts. The killer had smothered Griggs then, disturbed, had battered Martha to death as soon as she entered the house. The killing of Griggs worried Storer considerably. It meant that someone was on to him. Whoever killed Griggs had done so to prevent him telling Storer what he had discovered. What had Griggs dug up then: the identity of Rena's accomplice? The whereabouts of the briefcase? Fair enough! Storer thought, but what had Henry told the killer before he died. What other information had he run across – about Storer, about where Rena was hiding out? About Kathy Arden and Ma MacAusland? Storer closed his mind on the possibilities, slamming the lid on panic before it got the better of him.

He returned to the living-room and stood under the light shade studying every nook and cranny intently. Henry's pockets had been emptied but nothing else had been disturbed. That meant that the killer was satisfied he had suppressed the information, had got something in the wallet or diary, enough to allay his need for a further search. What the hell was it? Storer took the Gold Flake packet from the table and systematically tore it open. Of course there was no message inked inside the flap. He put the remains of the packet down again, then paused. On the table was a copy of *Engine*. Griggs had never owned a car in his life. To the best of Storer's knowledge he had no interest at all in things mechanical. Maybe a kindly neighbour had lent him the magazine. Storer examined the date on the cover: the issue could not have been on the stand more than a couple of days. He threw it down on the carpet by Henry's slippers and dropped on all fours over it like a schoolboy at a comic paper. Flicking the pages slowly he worked from front cover to back. The torn half-page was evident, done neatly along a deliberate fold. Storer got up, rolled the magazine and slipped it into his pocket. For a moment he stared down at Henry again. Griggs was the last of his foster-father's mates; and, so the story had it, the best singer in the business. Neither Griggs nor his missus need worry about the future now. The killer had saved Storer a hundred quid. Storer wished he hadn't.

He opened the outer door cautiously, brought in the two pint bottles of milk and laid them clear of the blood puddle in the hall. He let himself out into the corridor and gingerly closed the door behind him, matching the broken edge and patting it down. The corridor was still empty when he pushed through the wired-glass door to his right and hurried down the fire stairs and out by the back way. The sun was still shining and the paintwork of the Porsche gleamed like a red jewel by the kerbside of Brankscombe Row. But up-river the cloud bar had come closer: it was no longer paper-flat but had shape and solidity now, like a carding of black wool. Storer shivered again, climbed into the Porsche and drove swiftly off in search of a newsagent's stand.

2

The sign over the car lot said MAURICE FORTUNE in crude orange painted letters. Two jerry-built offices and an elongated nissen-hut tried to huddle under the sign as if the five-foot-high letters, the power of the name, would lend them a status they did not deserve. In front of the yard was a small service station spoiled by a repetition of Fortune's name in the same gigantic script and hue plastered all over it. Storer took the car along the black path to the front of the pumps and sat there looking up at the squat shapes as if they were alien robots. *Maurice Fortune: Spares & Service, All Makes. Sole Distributor,* so the advertisement in the magazine told him. It did not tell him what Fortune was the sole distributor of; from the assembled models lined and ticketed within the yard Storer could gather no clue. He sat waiting five minutes, then rapped the horn once more. Out of the smallest shed sauntered a young man. He had oil on his hands and acne on his chin, wore brown coveralls stained with grease, and had brown hair no cleaner than the swab of cotton waste in his hand. Storer took him to be no older than twenty but he walked up like a veteran. He came over, casting the swab away casually.

'Yer?' the boy said. 'How many?'

'How many what?'

'Gallons.'

'No,' said Storer. 'I don't want petrol.'

'Whatcher want then?'

'I'm looking for Mr Fortune.'

'Aint 'ere.'

'Where can I find him?'

'What's yer problem?'

The boy studied the Porsche with careful expertise, but kept all trace of admiration out of his face. Perhaps he did not appreciate Continental cars.

'I'd rather tell it to Mr Fortune,' said Storer. 'When will he be back?'

'Gawd knows,' said the boy.

Storer got out of the car. The boy backed off a couple of paces, leaving a single dirty paw print on the car roof. Storer wondered if the kid was used to menace emerging from the vehicles which stopped there.

'I thought we might talk about a trade-in price for the car here,' Storer said.

'This?' said the boy. 'Yer want t'trade 'er in?'

'Yeah,' said Storer. 'What've you got to offer?'

The boy pursed his lips and the whole bottom half of the face followed. The cold made his pimples stand out like old bullet wounds. He stared at Storer then at the car, suspiciously.

'Are you the only one here?' Storer asked, looking up the yard.

'Yer,' said the boy indignantly.

Storer sighed. 'Well, I don't expect you to give me a valuation. Tell you what, let me see what you've got back there. If anything takes my fancy then I'll drop round tomorrow and have a chat with Mr Fortune. He will be around tomorrow, will he?'

'Should be.' The boy stood aside and fell in step with Storer who walked under the sign and up the yard. The price cards were Scotch-taped to the windscreens. They looked high to Storer, but he was no expert. He said, 'You wouldn't care to call Fortune now and make an appointment for me?'

'Nope.'

'I don't suppose the boss tells you where he's going, is that it?'

The boy bridled. 'Yer, I know where he's at. He just wouldn't want t'be disturbed.'

'Not even for business?'

'Not even for business,' said the boy. 'How come I aint seen you round 'ere before?'

'I've never been around here before,' Storer said.

He took the mint copy of *Engine* from his pocket and held it out as a visual aid to explanation. 'I saw your advert and decided you might be able to help. Seems I was wrong?'

'Maybe you were,' the boy said. 'Whatcher after?'

'Something big and fast with lots of muscle,' Storer said.

'Faster than what you got?'

'I need more weight,' Storer said.

'American,' the boy said. 'Weight and power.'

'How about a Mercedes?' said Storer.

'Got none.'

'Or a Ventora?'

'No real muscle in a Ventora,' the boy said after a pause. 'How about this then?'

Storer paused in front of the Bonneville with the left-hand drive. It looked the worse for wear and the price was ridiculous.

'It might do,' he said. He took a step closer to the boy and motioned to him. 'The real reason I came here, is I want to do a fast trade-in. I want to do it to-night. I want rid of the Porsche. You . . . got me?'

The boy grinned like a fox in a hen-run. 'I gotcher.'

'Couldn't we go into the office and you phone up Mr Fortune and ask him to sally over here?'

'Nothin' doin',' the boy said adamantly. 'Hey, who sent you? I know all the . . . geezers in this trade.'

'Nobody sent me,' Storer said. He smiled at the boy. 'And you don't know everybody in this trade, kid, because you don't know me.'

He reached out fast and caught the boy by the left arm and doubled it over like a length of worn hose. He put his knee against the base of the boy's spine, finding the bone easily under the scant flesh, and pushed.

Then, lifting the lightweight on the locked arm, he shoved him over to the open door of the office and, using the boy's chest as a ram, broke through the door. The boy struggled. His breath made puffs of condensation like the explosions of small bombs in the air as he bucked and plunged against the confining hold. Storer bore down on the arm, then with a flick of his wrists shot the boy across the office against a filing cabinet.

'I got no lolly 'ere, mister,' the boy yelled. 'Aint nothin' 'ere worth floggin'.'

'The Ventora,' Storer said. He caught the boy by the front of the coveralls and yanked him to his feet. 'Who brought it and who took it away?'

'I don't know nothin' about no Ventora.'

'Talk.'

'I'm tellin' yer, I don't know . . .'

'All right,' said Storer. 'Where's the boss, where's Fortune, right now, right this minute?'

'Christ, I don't know.'

'Come on, George Washington,' Storer said, racking him against the edge of the cabinet. 'Tell me before I kill you.'

'I don't know.'

Storer pinched the zipper of the coveralls and drew it all the way down, exposing a grubby woollen sweater and a pair of soiled jockey shorts. He peeled the coveralls back to pin the boy's arms and leaned on him. With his left forearm around his head, Storer's fingers squeezed the mouth. 'Are you going to tell me?'

The boy shook his head. His eyes were dilated with fear. Storer could feel his teeth gnawing against the hard edge of his palm. He pushed tighter and hooked his right hand into the sagging yoke of the coveralls. The boy's scream was muffled, but shrill enough to set up a vibration in Storer's wrist.

'Now,' Storer said, slackening both grips. 'Tell me.'

Though his breath came out in a freezing cloud the boy's face was bathed with sweat and the rank smell of his terror and agony wafted across Storer.

'I don't . . .' the boy whined.

Storer moved in with the right hand again. The boy thrashed and squirmed but just before Storer screwed on the pressure he nodded. Storer eased his left hand and the boy jerked his head to one side. 'I'll tell you. Jesus, mister, I'll tell you.'

'Talk.'

'He's round the corner with a bird: a fancy-piece. He knocks 'er off regular – in the afternoon, so's his wife won't know,' the boy gasped.

'Address.'

'I don't know accurate,' the boy pleaded. 'Round the corner second left past the 'ospital. Gideon Street, third house, top-floor.'

'What's her name?'

'Dawson,' the boy stuttered. 'Cilla Dawson.'

Storer slackened off. 'How do you know so much?'

Doubling over the remnants of his pain, the boy hung his head. 'I been there an' all,' he said. 'Night-time, see.'

Storer shifted to the telephone, traced the cable down and ripped it from the wall point. When he turned again the boy was coming at him with a jack-handle. Savage fury gnarled his young face. He was showing more guts than Storer imagined. Storer swayed away from the blow. The heavy rod hissed past his shoulder by a hairsbreadth and crunched into the desk-top. The boy went after it. Storer clipped him twice on the side of the head and he went down over the desk, slid over on to the floor and lay motionless, belly down. Storer walked off and left him there.

3

Rena Rushton said, 'I don't know where Storer is. He never tells me where he goes. He simply stalks out and that's the last I see of him until he knocks on my door again.'

She glanced nervously along the wedge of Baker Street which was visible from the call-box. Now that the sun had gone her dark glasses seemed more of an affectation than ever, but she kept them on, peering at all the shadowy figures who passed by the corner.

'What d'you mean, he might be on to us? I thought you were handling that side of it?' she said. She paused, then exclaimed, 'You can't be sure! All right, all right, I'll send the telegram today, if that's what you want. I doubt if Storer *will* like it. He'd rather act slowly, give Rushton time to . . . No, I agree. I agree. The faster we move in now the better for all of us. Will Rushton . . .?'

She slipped the glasses down her nose to inspect a man who loitered on the corner not far from the box; it was no one she could identify. She fumbled a cigarette from her purse and struck the match, listening all the while to the voice on the phone.

'Are we going to give him back the accounts?' she said, then, 'Yes, yes, I suppose it would be asking for real trouble not to play ball. I take your point. But what about Storer and my sister, and this woman he's saddled us with?'

The man on the corner glared at her. He was fifty if he was a day and dressed in an old-fashioned morning suit with a hairy black bowler perched on the wings of his grey hair. He had a leather brief-case, well scuffed, under his arm but no umbrella. Rena stared back at him, daring him to rap on the glass. She had only been in the box five minutes.

'Oh!' she said. 'All of them? No, no, it makes no difference to me. I don't care who you kill.' She sucked smoke into her lungs nervously, and expelled it through her nostrils. 'All three of them if you like. Yes, I agree. It is safer that way.'

The man in the bowler was coming towards her. She eyed him over the top of her glasses. For a hideous moment she thought he might have a gun in his pocket or a bomb in the brief-case, but he only hovered outside, scowling rudely at her. Carefully she turned her back on him, using the gesture not only as an insolent rebuff but to steel her nerve. She listened some more to the voice on the wire, nodding impatiently as if to a lesson she had already mastered.

'I'll manage that part of it all right,' she said, 'but the rest is up to you. Yes, I'll be careful. You be careful too.' In a tone as cold and unyielding as a brass rod, she said, 'I love you,' and hung up.

When she emerged from the call-box the bowler-hat brushed past her, muttering, 'Damn' chatterin' women.'

She stepped back, gave a discreet but obscene suggestion with her fingers, then hurried off down Baker Street to the Gresham to await Storer's return.

On the way she stopped off at a post office and composed a long and expensive telegram to her husband. In it she informed him that the price of silence had suddenly shot up to a quarter of a million in hand-picked gems. She sucked the pen, trying to imagine what it would be like to be rich, rich in her own right, but could not. Instead she imagined how pleasurable it would be to see her sister die, and Storer too. Come to think of it, especially Storer. If there was one thing she hated it was a man she could not control.

4

Storer hit the door with his foot. It flew inwards. He had the gun in his hand and, in spite of the scene which met his eyes, held it steady, pointed straight at the bed.

'Maurice Fortune?'

'What the hell . . .?'

'Are you Maurice Fortune?'

'Yer, but . . .'

Storer shifted the gun to his left hand and leapt forward.

'Jeezus!' Maurice Fortune cried when Storer hauled him out from between the girl's legs. 'Can't a man have any privacy!'

He blinked up at Storer from the tops of his eyeballs, but Storer had no difficulty in pinning him. The car-dealer must have felt particularly vulnerable spread-eagled across the bed-end, naked as a babe. The girl, a dyed-blonde, clawed across him and Maurice judiciously cocked his hip to prevent her knees digging into soft portions of his anatomy and doing him damage. She got herself across to the bed-head and cowered against it. Storer told her to stop where she was and she did so, gripping the sheet for protection. Maurice Fortune had a cool head and the point of his afternoon's exercise had not been wholly lost, but when Storer increased pressure on his windpipe fear must have squirted suddenly into him for after an instant his body quit bragging and went slack.

'Whatever it is you think I done,' Maurice said. 'I didn't.'

Maurice Fortune was a comic figure stripped. Putting on beef in all the wrong places, with brittle reddish hair, he resembled an out-of-work rugby league player rubbed down by too many brutal scrums. When he swallowed the taut skin shoved his Adam's apple into his gullet.

'A brand-new Ventora, Maurice,' Storer said. 'Who brought it and who took it away?'

'Ventora,' he said. 'Vauxhall Ventora. Never handled one of those.'

'Come on.'

'If you're interested in buying, I'd be prepared to do business in a more orthodox . . .'

Storer bore down. Maurice squirmed but did not have the flexibility to fling his legs back. In spite of the slicking of sweat on the man's skin Storer's hold was solid.

'Fancy a broken back, Maurice?' Storer enquired. 'It's pretty painful making love in any position with a broken back.'

'You wouldn't,' Maurice said. He simpered. 'Would you?'

'Wouldn't I!' Storer said.

'Good God, I believe you would,' Maurice said.

'Information,' Storer said. 'That's all I want.'

The room was shabby but comfortably furnished, and in the new TV set and transistor radio and in the elegant bed itself Storer could see the cost of Maurice Fortune's recreation. The girl looked vicious to him, mean, and she was strongly built, though not even slightly pretty. She started to bellow suddenly, but sounds of that sort were probably commonplace in this block. She bellowed like a cow with flies on her tail. Storer told Maurice to tell her to stop. The dealer did so and the girl went back to whimpering quietly.

'You realise,' Maurice said, 'that I could get into sad straits by telling you?'

'You're in sad straits now, friend.'

'True,' Maurice said. 'It was brought in by a woman 'bout two weeks ago. She gave me forty quid to garage and service it.'

'What did she look like?'

'A . . . blonde, rather . . . voluptuous. Well tricked out, expensive gear like. Not a dolly-bird; mature. She'd be around twenty-eight or thirty.'

'She didn't give you a name?'

'No, sir.'

'You didn't ask?'

'You're obviously a man of the world,' Maurice said. 'Why should I ask if she don't want to tell?'

'It's not in the yard now,' Storer said.

'You're right. It was collected this morning.'

'What time?'

'Nine, nine-thirty.'

'By whom?'

'A man. He gave me another fiver.'

'I take it you didn't know him?'

Maurice hesitated briefly. His flesh was flushed like a scald. 'I know him,' he admitted. 'Are you connected?'

'His name.'

Maurice licked his lips. 'You won't say I told you, will you?'

'Hurry, or you won't be fit to tell anyone anything, Fortune.'

'Well, it was Burchill. Roy Burchill. He works for a man called Rushton. Maybe you've . . .'

'I've heard of him,' Storer said.

'I really don't want to have the organisation on . . .'

Storer let him go. Maurice swung round on the bed and propped himself against the pillow, scratching at the welts Storer's fingers had left on his shoulders and neck.

Storer said, 'If I were you, Maurice, I'd keep my trap shut about this.'

'Oh, I will, sir,' Maurice assured him. 'I surely will.'

'If you don't,' Storer said, hoisting the gun a little higher, 'I'll kill you. Clear?'

'Abundantly,' Maurice said.

When Storer left, Maurice was patting the blonde's thigh as if she was a poodle. Though he was comforting her, Storer could tell that his heart wasn't in it. He knew he could trust Fortune not to call Burchill and report the visit. Maurice might be cool on the outside but inside he was scared sick and, being scared, he was cautious. The scared ones usually survived. Storer was scared too now but not for himself. He was scared for Ma and Kathy Arden. He ran down the dank staircase to the street and dived into the Porsche.

5

It was snowing in Watford. The cloud had chosen that area on which to unburden itself in a trial run for the blizzard it had saved for London. By the time Storer got there, dusk was beginning to drift down and he was tensed up almost to snapping point by the effort of holding the car near its limit on the bad road surfaces.

No lights showed in the front of the house. He let himself in with the yale key which had been his since his fifteenth birthday. There was no sound inside. Storer paused in the darkened hallway at the bottom of the stairs for a long time listening before he took the gun out and climbed up the straight flight. He balanced his weight on his heels and let his soles slide gingerly on to the creaking boards. When he reached the landing he paused again. He could hear voices now from inside the back room. He stepped forward and flung open the door. Ma MacAusland dropped her cards and pressed her hand to her bosom.

'Och, my God, Storer, what a fright y'gave me.'

The room no longer looked like a left-luggage office. It was cosy; the electric heater at full blast, the lamp shining warm light on the table. A tray with tea-things occupied the top of the dresser. On the table drawn up between them was a colourful scattering of playing cards and a cribbage board. The girl stared at him mutely and it was no longer like seeing Rena there. He wondered why he had ever thought they could get away with it.

'Are you all right?' Storer asked.

'Of course we're all right,' Ma said indignantly. She referred to the girl. 'Sure w'are?'

'Fine,' the girl said, uncertainly.

Storer sighed and relaxed.

'You look whacked,' Ma said. She got up. 'Take this seat.'

'No trouble?' asked Storer, as he seated himself at the table.

'No bother at all,' said Ma. Storer noted the brief conspiratorial glance which the woman exchanged with the girl and knew there had been trouble. It was amicable enough now, Kathy passive and quiet in spite of her obvious apprehension. 'Should there've been trouble?'

'No,' Storer replied. To the girl he said, 'Are you okay?'

'Yes.'

The pause was full of awkwardness: even Storer was embarrassed by the unspoken questions. He got up and took Ma by the arm.

'I want to talk to you,' he said. 'Downstairs.'

'Right y'are then,' Ma said. She followed Storer down into the living-room which was in its customary state of disorder.

'Cup of tea, Storer?'

He shook his head. It was cold in the room, for the fire had died. He fished a handful of coal lumps from the bucket and flung them on the smouldering ashes, stirring them with the toe of his shoe. 'How soon could you be out of here?'

'Eh?'

'You and the girl both,' said Storer. 'Pack a couple of cases and let's go.'

'Now see here . . .'

'Unless you'd rather be dead.'

The big woman slumped slowly to the cushion of

the chair. She jerked her thumb at the ceiling. 'You're not planning on killing her, Storer?'

'No.'

'I wouldn't stand for that.'

'Remember Henry and Martha Griggs?'

'Ay, but what . . .'

'They're dead,' Storer said.

The woman's eyes shrivelled to the size of raisins but she did not cry. Storer had never seen her cry. In the new print frock she looked ten years younger but even as he watched he saw age creep slowly over her again. She seemed to swell with the shocked grief that his news had incurred.

'You didn't . . .'

'Of course not,' said Storer. 'Listen, Ma, I've . . . I've got into something I can't get out of. Listen, I *was* supposed to put Kathy down, but . . .'

'Over my dead body.'

The tension in him flared into anger and he leapt from the chair, shouting, 'Christ, woman, I'm not trying to *kill* her, I'm *trying* to keep her alive. Her and you too, you stupid old cow.'

'Sit down, Storer,' she said with surprising mildness. 'An' don't be callin' me a stupid old thingummy again.'

Storer contained himself, but the restlessness and urgency were like a fever in him. He paced across the length of the rug and back again, knowing that she was watching him.

'I'm sorry, Ma,' he said. 'But *somebody's* got to trust me. I don't want you on my conscience too.'

'Tell me about it.'

'No,' said Storer. 'I can't. The less you know the better. Anyway, we don't have time.'

'Is it that sister of hers? Are you in cahoots with her?'

'I was,' Storer said, 'but I'm not now. I'm on my own now, all on my own.'

'I can't just pack up an' leave,' Ma said. 'How long'll it be for?'

'Not long,' Storer said. It was his turn to point to the ceiling. 'Will she trust you?'

'I don't rightly know,' Ma said.

'You looked cosy enough.'

'Ay, but you're back, an' the last time she clapped eyes on you, Storer, she wound up dunted on the noddle and kidnapped. She'll not exactly be disposed t'take your word on anything now.'

'Dammit,' said Storer softly. 'I'll have to get her co-operation.'

'Is somebody really after us?' Ma asked.

'Yeah,' said Storer. He made another brief tour of the limits of the carpet, rubbing his hand under the collar of the sheepskin coat and massaging his neck muscles. 'I should never have dragged you into it.'

'But y'couldn't find anybody else t'trust?' Ma said.

'That's right,' Storer said. 'I thought I had it all under control.'

'And all y'had t'do was kill the girl?'

'Something like that,' Storer replied.

'Have y'killed before?'

He turned to face her, staring into the sad eyes: then he said, 'Yes.'

'Women?'

'No, never.'

'Is that the truth?'

'Yeah.'

'Your Daddy killed too once,' Ma said. 'I'm meanin'

Alex. He killed once in self-defence, but he always said he would never kill a woman.'

'Ma,' Storer said. 'Ask her to trust me. Tell her to do exactly as I say and she'll come to no harm.'

'Ach, Storer, you can't give'r that guarantee.'

'No, I can't,' Storer admitted.

'How much are you playin' for, son?'

'I'm not playing now,' said Storer. 'I just want out.'

'But you know too much, is that it?'

'Far too much. I'm in the middle,' said Storer, 'and the stake's a quarter million . . .'

'A quarter mill . . .'

'A lot of people will kill any number of women to get their hands on that amount.'

'Ay,' said Ma. 'You're right. Where are y'takin' us then?'

'London,' Storer said. 'I'll put you up in an hotel. Do you really think you can persuade her I'm on the level?'

Ma slapped her hands on her thighs and pushed herself to her feet. 'I'll try,' she said. 'It won't be easy but I'll try.'

'How long will it take you to be packed and ready?'

'An hour at most.'

'Fine,' said Storer.

'Is it . . . them's killed Henry and Martha?'

'Yeah,' said Storer. 'And they might be on their way here now.'

'Right, son,' the woman said. She reached up and rumpled his hair. He did not stop her. She grinned stiffly, with an effort at warmth. 'I'll take your word for it. Anyway, I'm far too young t'die.'

Storer listened to her clumping upstairs again, then he went to the kitchen to hunt through the larder for the whisky. Now he had Ma on his side he felt a lot better. He had told her the truth too, more or less. He no longer wanted to play Rena's game. All he wanted was out with a whole skin – and maybe fifty thousand pounds. He found the whisky in the bread-tin and poured a stiff shot into a cup. Carrying cup and bottle he went back to the living-room and stretched himself in the armchair with his frozen toes out to the springing flames of the fire.

When Ma and the girl came down with the suitcases half an hour later, Storer was fast asleep.

6

The river was a black line defined by new fallen snow. Beyond it the elms lifted their branches to detain the last few drifting flakes as if they too sought the white warmth of a snow coat. The curtains in the study were not drawn and the view was like a quiet picture which Mills, in all good taste, had deliberately constructed for the pleasure of his guests. Behind closed doors across the vast expanse of the wood-floored hall the dinner party was going on quite merrily without its host. The host had more pressing matters on hand, though he had promoted himself to brandy and cigars and seen to it that his uninvited guests had been furnished with the necessary comforts. Mills was a small man in his middle forties. Even in a tuxedo he looked like an actor only recently graduated from juvenile roles. He wore owlish glasses. To a stranger the cigar might seem an affectation of success but Mills smoked them all the time. He sat back now in an armchair of apple-green leather and surveyed the three men with indulgent amusement.

Marquand was off to the left in a matching armchair, nursing a diminutive china coffee cup in his huge elegant hands. Marquand's suit was dove-grey and his legs, as long as stilts, stuck far out in front of him. Instead of growing fat with prosperity, Marquand had become leaner, his meaty features refining themselves until almost all trace of the working-class town-hall boxer had vanished. In recent years he had achieved a rough-hewn but perfectly acceptable handsomeness to link in with his cultivated plum-in-the-mouth accent. The other two men were not at ease: Rushton especially was nervous. Burchill stood by the window, from which position he could watch each of the others.

Four years ago Mills had married the daughter of an earl. For his second fling at wedlock Marquand had picked himself a member of the Italian aristocracy who had starred in a few small budget movies. Rushton envied them: he had never quite succeeded in emulating their graciousness. This evening, however, he had no room for envy, only for a kind of fawning gratitude which Marquand, like Mills, regarded with suppressed contempt.

'Did you expect us to refuse?' Mills asked.

'Well, I didn't know,' said Rushton, flushing. 'I didn't think you'd be able to rake-up that many diamonds in just twenty-four hours.'

'That side of the organisation is highly efficient,' Mills said. 'Isn't it, Paul?'

'I like to think so,' Marquand said. 'But then it's not for me to say.'

'You're both taking it very calmly,' said Rushton.

'Would you rather we got excited?' said Mills. He puffed on the cigar to re-enliven the coal at the tip. 'It was on the cards, wasn't it? After you bungled the delivery last time, it was only a matter of time before they put the knife in deep. I must admit I am rather surprised they didn't hold off a little longer, or be a little less ambitious in their claim.'

'I . . . I hope,' said Rushton, 'they do return the accounts.'

'Hm!' said Marquand. 'It would seem that if they are rooking us for a quarter of a million they *will* play fair. It must be obvious to them, to your lady wife at least, that the syndicate simply can't afford to lash out any more. It's been an expensive mistake, Rushton.'

'I know.'

'And you will be obliged to repay the organisation,' said Mills.

'Of course; yes, I know.'

'Even if it means liquidating some of your personal assets.'

'I don't have . . .'

'Gradually,' said Mills. 'I'm sure we're not going to be *too* unreasonable. Are we, Paul?'

'Oh, not really,' said Marquand. 'You can brace up some of your corporations, Rushton. Been a shade slack lately, some of them. Not operating at full potential.'

'I'll . . . revise now,' Rushton promised. He no longer thought of them as partners or as upstarts, but saw them – so great was his relief – as benefactors. 'I'll really wade in. I have some ideas which I'd like approved. Some . . .'

'Later,' Mills said. 'First we must work out just how this ransom is to be paid and how best we can protect it. I take it I can leave the clearance to you, Paul. You might well be able to trace the stones when they come on the market again.'

'I shouldn't be surprised,' said Marquand. 'It would be better, of course, to arrange *not* to have them lifted in the first place.'

'I wonder why she picked Grassleigh Common,' said Rushton. 'It's a long way to go to make the exchange.'

The map lay colourful on the table-top near Mills's foot. He cocked his head slightly to look at it. 'It seems obvious,' he said, 'that Grassleigh Common has all the qualities she, or *they* I should say, require. They'll have some elaborate arrangement for picking up the diamonds and clearing out before we can do anything.'

'If I was setting it up, I'd use a helicopter,' Marquand said.

'Of course you would,' said Mills. 'That's just what we'll do in fact. We'll hire a helicopter.'

'I'd make it two, if I were you,' Burchill put in.

'Two helicopters then,' Mills agreed. 'We can control the cars on the ground from there and use radio to communicate with each other.'

'It means,' said Rushton, 'that the Common itself will be clear.'

'I think,' said Mills, lifting the telegram and unfurling it as if it was a scroll of papyrus, 'that we should be obedient to the letter. Two men of our choosing in one car to circle the Common. One man to come forward with the diamonds . . .'

'And the money,' put in Rushton. 'Fifty thousand.'

'Yes, and the money,' said Mills, 'and effect the exchange. I suppose it'll take a little while to check off the contents.'

Marquand got up to help himself to more brandy from the liquor trolley. He mused over it, then lifted the map from the table and held it across his arm while he consulted the relevant area. 'We'd better be careful,' he said. 'I wouldn't want them to pull the same stunt as they did at the Museum.'

'No,' said Mills. 'It was humiliating, not to say distressing, to fall for that hoary old trick. However, this time...'

'Who goes?' said Burchill. He looked directly at Rushton. 'Do you intend to be one of them?'

'Me?' said Rushton. 'Well, I . . . it doesn't specifically ask for me on the instructions, so perhaps . . .'

'A young man would be best,' said Marquand. 'Fast and alert and clued in.'

'I don't suppose,' said Burchill, 'you'd trust me again.'

'Oh, yes,' said Mills amicably. 'I assumed you'd be the man with the consignment. But we need another.'

'Storer,' said Rushton.

'Hm!' Marquand said dubiously. 'I'd rather keep it within the organisation.'

'What do you think, Roy?' Mills asked.

'I think,' said Burchill slowly, 'that Storer would do very well. The less the boys know about this transaction the better. Storer is a born loner. He's always discreet.'

'But is he the man we really want?' said Marquand.

'They're your diamonds,' Rushton said. 'Do you want one of yours along as a protection?'

'No,' said Marquand, suddenly making up his mind. 'No, it's too risky using one of our own for the transporter. We'd have to fill him in and . . .' He shrugged.

Mills nodded. 'Very well. Storer it shall be. If he agrees.'

'Storer will do anything if the price is right,' Burchill said.

Rushton gave a sigh of relief. 'I appreciate all your trouble,' he said. 'It's good to have people you can depend on at a time like this.'

'Yes,' said Mills. 'Still, I do think we should keep it to ourselves, don't you? I mean, Browning and Lenihan might not agree and one thing we can't afford at the moment is delay.'

'Shouldn't we have a meeting?' Rushton said. 'They might not like the idea of all that cash going off without their approval.'

'Diamonds aren't their business,' Mills said. 'Besides I'm confident we'll manage to put a spoke in your wife's wheel – if you know what I mean – and save ourselves the diamonds *and* all the fuss of grovelling for the return of the briefcase.' He took a golden pencil from the inner pocket of his dinner jacket and Burchill came forward with a notebook. 'No reason why we shouldn't plan out the positioning now. We'll have a discreet look at this Common tomorrow and finalise things. Can I leave that to you, Roy?'

'Of course.'

'I'll arrange the helicopters and cars. Marquand will have the diamonds ready and you, Rushton, the money.' He wrote the items down in small print, then looked up. 'Any questions?'

Brooding over the inch of brandy in his glass, Marquand murmured. 'I'm still not sure about Storer.'

'He always delivers,' Mills said. 'He's done top work for all of us at one time or another. Besides, Roy will be in the car with him, and we can trust Roy to keep a close hand on the deal. Can't we, Roy?'

'Yes,' said Burchill. 'I can handle Storer.'

Mills laughed. 'I'm sure you can,' he said. He raised his almost empty glass. 'Sunday: may all go well.'

'Sunday,' Marquand said.

For the first time in months, Rushton managed to smile.

7

Shortly after midnight Storer parked the Porsche in Wilcox Square and hurried through the snow to the Gresham. The drifting flakes were small and fine but so dry they did not adhere to his coat. Their myriad shadows filled each pocket of light with movement, and they had already coated the streets thickly enough to muffle the sounds of late-night traffic. The breeze of a passing car swirled up a cloud of snow-dust like a miniature storm as Storer climbed the steps of the hotel.

He went directly up the dimly-lighted staircase to Rena's room. It took her several minutes to answer his knocking. He kept his hand in his pocket on the gun. She was in her nightdress, her body showing through it against the light.

'Oh, God, Storer,' she complained, admitting him. 'I was sound asleep.'

He went in carefully, making the woman screen him. The room was empty. He realised that he was acting melodramatically but nevertheless crossed to the curtains and parted them.

'Polonius, he left,' Rena said. She sat down on the

bed and lit herself a cigarette. 'What's that in your pocket? Not a gun, not a real live gun.'

'Shut up,' said Storer. He came over and took her arm just under the elbow and held it. 'I want the brief-case, and I want it now.'

'Oh, a tough cookie,' Rena said. 'What's got you all riled?'

'The deal is crumbling, Rena,' he said. 'And I don't want to get caught under the rubble.'

She pulled away from him angrily. 'Don't give me your worries, Storer,' she said. 'And don't try to con me. The deal is perfect. I sent the telegram today. It's all set up.'

'When?'

'Sunday,' she said. 'Morning.'

'And where?'

'Grassleigh Common, down near Sevenoaks.'

'Whose idea was it to fire off the telegram?'

'Mine,' she said. 'All mine. I'm sick of festering in this dump.'

'Can't you even exercise a little patience for your money,' said Storer. 'Why Grass . . .? What is it?'

'Grassleigh,' she said.

'Why this common? It'll be wide open and deserted on a Sunday morning.'

'That's what I want,' Rena said.

'Am I still to be delivery boy?'

'Of course.'

'And kill your sister?'

'That *was* the agreement.'

'Do your . . . friends know about Kathy?'

'Naturally.'

'I don't believe you, Rena. With a quarter million riding on it they aren't going to be too concerned with your hare-brained scheme to cover yourself. Maybe somebody is helping you with the rest but as far as the Kathy-bit goes that's your own idea.'

'It's all my own idea, Storer.'

'When did you send the telegram?'

'Around noon.'

'Marquand will never agree. Even if he is willing to bail Rushton out he won't be able to rake together two hundred and fifty thousand quidsworth of stones in a day and a half.'

'That's his problem.'

'I'm bloody sure he won't,' said Storer. 'You've run yourself into trouble. I don't see what the hurry . . .' He stopped. 'The contact?'

'Clever boy!'

'So I'm to kill your sister, fake it to look like your corpse and convince Burchill and Rushton I'm the right man for the job – all in twenty-four hours?'

'You can do it, Charlie Brown,' Rena said. She was in a strange mood: ebullient, almost skittish, as if she had collected aces from the draw. Storer too had aces in his hand, but he was beginning to wonder if he had enough of them.

'I want the briefcase, Rena.'

'No,' she said. 'I'll have it at the right place at the right time.'

'I suppose you're just going to walk up and hand it over,' Storer said. 'The syndicate's guns will be all over the county. They'll probably have a couple of whirlybirds up above. The syndicate would hire a battleship if they thought it would get you off their back and the accounts squared. They won't let it go as easily as they did last time. The last time was a candy-store caper compared to this.'

'Stop preaching,' Rena said. 'I have it all worked out. You and Burchill will be alone in the car with the money and the diamonds. You'll drive sedately towards Grassleigh only you won't stop there, you'll drive straight on.'

'To where?'

'I'll tell you that later,' said Rena.

'What about Burchill?'

'With your little revolver in his ribs he'll cooperate.'

'Then . . .'

'We'll have the swarm on our tail, but I reckon the Merk will outstrip them, particularly as you'll know the route and they won't.'

'And the helicopters?'

'Leave them to me,' Rena said. 'At a given point you'll ditch the car . . .'

'And Burchill with it?'

'Exactly,' Rena said. 'You'll climb over a fence and get into a Piper Cub.'

'Oh, God,' said Storer. 'All we need are the Men from UNCLE.'

'I'm serious,' Rena said. 'We get into a Piper Cub, you and I and the diamonds and buzz off into the wide blue yonder.'

'I suppose you've a pilot's licence.'

'I'll have a pilot whom I can trust,' said Rena. 'The 'copters can't match the speed of a Cub, nor do they have the range to follow us for long. By the time the syndicate gets organised we'll be well away.'

'There's only one small snag,' Storer said.

'What's that?'

'I'm not doing it.'

'Two hundred and fifty thous . . .'

‘A dream,’ said Storer. ‘A big pink dream, dear.’

‘Storer, I . . .’

‘Forget it,’ Storer said. ‘I don’t quite know what you have up your sleeve, but I don’t want any part of that crazy scheme.’

‘Bold, Storer, but not crazy.’

‘You still want me to kill Kathy?’

‘*Yes . . .*’

‘All right,’ said Storer. ‘I’ll kill her, but I want the briefcase. I’ll trade you Kathy for the briefcase.’

Rena laughed.

Storer said, ‘If you think you can sneak a couple of your accomplices up to Watford, better think again. She isn’t there now: neither is my mother. I . . . took the precaution . . .’

‘Bastard.’

‘. . . of removing them and hiding them somewhere . . . safe.’

‘Bastard, Storer.’

‘I’m not interested in blackmail,’ said Storer. ‘That’s not why I want your bloody briefcase. I just want to share your insurance. With that briefcase in my protection, then neither you nor Rushton is going to do me in without a very, very good reason.’

‘I don’t care,’ she said. ‘I won’t tell you where it is.’

‘No,’ said Storer, ‘and you can’t go whining to your comrades either, because they don’t know about your little private deal with me, do they?’

‘You really are a prime . . .’

‘Excuse me,’ said Storer. ‘I’m going now.’

‘What? Where?’

‘I don’t know,’ said Storer. ‘Out. Somewhere.’

‘You mean, you’re quitting,’ she said. ‘You’re quitting with only ten thousand?’

'Ten thousand isn't bad,' said Storer. 'At least I'm alive.'

'I told you before . . .'

'Uh-huh,' said Storer. 'But you didn't tell me everything. I'm supposed to be the man with the white cross on his chest, the pigeon. Well, I don't like the role. You can go stuff it up your garter, Rena.'

'You don't want to kill Kathy?'

'Why should I?'

'What about the rest of it?'

Storer shook his head. 'Rushton won't have me, that's for sure.'

'But if he agrees to let you make the exchange?'

'Are you really serious about all that Piper Cub rigmarole?'

'It's all arranged.'

'Then I'd think about it,' said Storer.

'Go to see Rushton. Pretend you're innocent.'

'Innocent!' said Storer. 'That's one part I can mock-up.'

'Let him ask you. He might, you know.'

'There's no danger,' Storer said. 'No danger at all.'

He left her then, going out quickly. He knew that before he was halfway downstairs she would be on the phone to Burchill. He thought of tapping the switchboard in the little office in the basement, but it would be on direct line at this hour and anyway he had no need to listen to Burchill and Rena's private yap. He already knew everything it was necessary for him to know: everything.

8

Rushton wakened from a fitful nightmare in which he had been robbing a jeweller's shop window and had been trapped by an iron gate crashing down on his wrists. He was, in the nightmare, both spectator and protagonist and had watched himself laughing, the dream mind shifting angles with the skill of a top film director, to add the agony of his own wicked laughter to the screams of his agonising imprisonment. The alarm bell was ringing and ringing overhead and he was pleading with the observer, also himself, to switch it off, but the observer only laughed louder. The bell brought him to consciousness again. Bathed in sweat, he realised he must have been awake for some time, eyes wide open, still caught in the dream. He was alone in the bedroom above the Stag's Palace, alone in the bed. He groped for the button of the lamp, found it and blinked against the light. He put on his glasses and stared around the room. Then he lifted the receiver.

'Who is it?' he said.

'Rushton?'

'Who's speaking?'

'Listen, Rushton, are you alone?'

'Is that you, Storer?'

'Yeah,' the voice said. 'Are you alone?'

'Well . . .' Rushton hesitated. He was alone, though just below there would still be some activity in the club. The bedside clock said it was 5 a.m. 'Yes, Storer, I'm alone.'

'No Burchill?' said Storer. 'No birds?'

'I told you, I'm quite alone.'

'All right,' said Storer. 'Can you get out of the Palace

without being seen? I mean without *anybody* seeing you, including Burchill.'

'What's all this about Bur . . . ?'

'Jesus, Rushton, can you?'

'I suppose so, if necessary, but . . .'

'Rushton,' Storer said, and a quality in the voice made Rushton's ire degenerate into mild panic. 'I'll pull up in Dean Street, outside the synagogue. You know it?'

'Yes, but . . .'

'I'll be there in fifteen minutes. I don't want to stop, so be on time.'

'But why?'

'I'll tell you in the car; a red Porsche,' said Storer. 'Just trust me, Rushton, and you won't regret it.'

'Have you found Rena?'

'Better than that,' said Storer.

'You . . . you've killed her?'

'No, I haven't killed her,' said Storer irritably.

'Wait,' said Rushton. 'If you won't give me some . . .'

'Don't twit around,' said Storer harshly. 'If you want to save your business and maybe your life, just be there. Okay?'

Rushton licked his parched lips. They tasted of the salt of the nightmare. He said, 'All right, Storer. I'll be there.'

'Fifteen minutes,' said Storer. 'And for God's sake don't let anyone see you.'

'Storer . . .'

Rushton was left with the dead receiver. He put it down, rubbed a hand across his chest and scratched his armpit. He could smell himself, the sweat, and it was like a sudden whiff of his own mortality. The notion of offering himself up alone to Storer in the middle of the night was unthinkable. It had been ten years since he had ventured alone into the streets of Soho either in daylight or after dark. Yet, as if hypnotised, he did as he had been told to do. He stripped and showered quickly and dressed himself in the most inconspicuous clothes he could find. Then, hurrying, he unlocked the bottom drawer of the desk in the living-room and from a green metal cash box took out a small Webley automatic. It was loaded. He checked the safety, then slipped it down into the silky depths of his overcoat pocket. Fifteen years at least since he had last carried a gun, twenty since he had used one. He went out into the corridor, locking the door behind him. He thought of using the elevator but changed his mind. Storer had been insistent: something about not telling Burchill. Troubled, Rushton made his exit discreetly by the back stairs and managed to escape from his own building without being seen. Five minutes later he was at the rendezvous and one minute later the red Porsche came fast out of Bateman Street and squealed to a halt at the kerb. Rushton felt breath pile up in his throat and his heart sit back upon itself as his whole body crouched for the bullet.

Storer opened the door of the Porsche. 'Get in, Rushton,' he said.

Rushton got in as fast as his trembling legs would carry him.

Storer took the car around the corner again and followed the small narrow streets out into Piccadilly.

'Well?' Rushton said.

Then Storer began to talk.

Gradually Rushton lost all sense of direction. He was sucked in by the words. Storer cut off his intermittent questions curtly, raising his voice and over-riding them, never once looking across at the old man who, with one hand braced against the dash, stared at the driver's face as if he was a devil steering him to hell. Only when Storer had been silent for over a minute did Rushton dare to speak.

'Good God, Storer. Do you expect me to believe this cock-and-bull story?'

'You'd better believe it,' Storer said.

'Believe that Roy is out to stab me in the back.'

'Yes.'

'And that Rena and he . . .'

'It's a hard life, Rushton,' Storer said. 'You can cry later. Right now I want to know what's in it for me if I get the case back and save your bacon. That's assuming you can persuade Marquand to risk a quarter of a million in diamonds.'

'But I have,' said Rushton abstractly. 'I mean he agreed.'

Storer grunted. 'He did, did he?'

'Why shouldn't he?'

'He thinks he can rake up a quarter of a million at thirty-six hours' notice,' said Storer. 'Who asked him?'

'I did.'

'Who else was there?'

'Roy and Mills.'

'Burchill and Mills,' said Storer. 'That's all?'

'And myself and Marquand, of course.'

The Porsche cut the King's Road corner at Sloane Square, the back end swinging viciously as the tyres dragged across the flurry of snow piled against the kerb. Storer straightened it up and took his foot off the gas a little, so that the car, after its fast lick from Soho, seemed to be crawling.

'Perhaps that explains it,' Storer said.

'Look here, Storer. I just can't take your word for it,' said Rushton. 'How do I know . . .?'

Storer said, 'Didn't it strike you as pretty damn' funny that Marquand, even Marquand, could lay his mitts on that amount of ice at such short notice? My God, there aren't many traders in Britain could do that.'

'He's got connections.'

'Yeah!'

'What are you implying, Storer?'

'The whole bloody thing's a carve-up,' said Storer. 'I should have realised it before. Jesus, these jokers aren't amateurs, yet they go into this like a bunch of schoolboys planning a raid on the larder. Browning and Lenihan weren't consulted?'

'No, Mills said . . .'

'Mills said they might be against it?'

'Yer.'

'Then it's a squeeze-play,' said Storer. 'It's Mills and Marquand and Burchill against you. It's their way of pushing you out.'

'A bullet would've been easier,' said Rushton.

'But that wouldn't have got rid of Lenihan and Browning too,' said Storer. 'Besides, they're not gangsters now. Yeah, they might hire a character like me from time to time to do their dirty work for them, but primarily they're respectable business men. Anyway to rub you out would damage the stability of the organisation, even with little old Roy waiting in the wings to step right into your shoes.'

'But what about the accounts?'

'I'm not sure,' Storer admitted. 'It's possible they're fakes.'

'I checked them myself.'

'Faked up to put you and Lenihan and Browning on the spot and leave the others free to move in on your side of things.'

'I don't understand much of this,' said Rushton in perplexity. 'My wife for instance . . .'

'They needed her as a blind,' said Storer. 'Or maybe it was all cooked up between her and Burchill. I don't know for sure either.'

'But to kill her sister . . .' Rushton shook his head. 'I can't believe it.'

'The question is,' Storer said, 'what you're going to do about it?'

'What can I do?'

'Go through with it,' said Storer. 'I'll be in the car with Burchill – right?'

'Yes, we'd agreed on that.'

'You did,' said Storer. 'Then for sure I'm marked as the patsy.'

'I can't take your word for it, Storer,' Rushton said. 'I need proof. Rena . . .'

'All right,' Storer said. He touched the brake pedal to bring the Porsche sliding to a halt. He executed a three-point turn across Kensington High Street and headed back towards the city centre. 'All right, Rushton, I'll give you the proof. In the meantime, listen, and I'll tell you what I'll do.'

'How much?' Rushton asked.

'Fifty thousand,' Storer said.

'Blackmail.'

'Come on, Rushton, I'm working to save your empire, and you don't think fifty thousand is a reasonable fee.'

'Yes,' Rushton said apologetically. 'Of course,

Storer. Of course it is. Give me proof, and I'll listen to more.'

Storer nodded grimly and pressed his foot down on the gas. The sleek red car hissed over the loose runner of snow which at that hour of the morning stretched empty and unsullied all the way back to the heart of London.

9

Kathy Arden could not sleep. She lay listening to the steady breathing of the woman in the adjacent bed. She wondered if she had gone completely mad, or if the whole thing was a nightmare from which she would wake eventually: the sudden night-ride from Watford, the big hushed London hotel, people around her and the man – most of all the man, grim and sad and silent. She could have pleaded with the clerk at reception or the porter or anyone to set her free, but somehow she was more afraid of being unprotected again than she was of him now.

Ma MacAusland trusted him and she, in a strange way, had come to trust Ma, to depend on her. She had never really been free, only lost, since her mother's death, and in the past few days, even with the shadow of fear and uncertainty on her, she had felt as if she had come out of a trance. She believed what the woman told her, that there were men out to kill her and that she was important. Important! She! Kathy Arden, who had never been out of the Midlands in her life and could count her acquaintances, never mind her friends, on the fingers of one hand. She was involved in something evil, but talk of death had no meaning for her. Her father had died before she was four years old and she could not remember him: the only death she had ever experienced was the slow dwindling away which her mother had gone through and which she had been forced to watch at close range. Death then had been a relief and she could not conceive of it being violent and sudden. Death was invidious, sly and vulgar and benefited no one. Her own death would benefit no one. It would make no one happy and no one sad – except perhaps Ma MacAusland. She felt that she meant something to the big Scots woman and, by reflection, meant something too to the man called Storer.

When she saw him asleep in the armchair he had looked so utterly worn out and helpless that she had felt the urge to care for him, as she might have wanted to care for an orphan child, but when he was awake he was strong and domineering and that also appealed to a latent instinct in her. It all added up to confusion: more especially now when she was no longer a prisoner. The telephone stood on the table by the bed: all she had to do to be free of these people was lift it and ask for the police. She could walk out of the door and downstairs. Even Ma MacAusland could not keep her prisoner in a large London hotel. She had to face the startling and abrupt fact that she remained here now of her own free will. That fact, she supposed, made her a prisoner of even more dangerous forces than menaced her from the outside world. If anything she was a victim of herself, of the lonely martyrdom which had consumed her youth. She turned restlessly on her hip and heard the woman rise up too, a stealthy rustle of sheets, to watch over her. The attention comforted her and flattered her too. She put her head on the huge smooth stiff-starched pillow and closed her eyes.

The telephone rang. Ma had it in her hand within a second and the lamp went on. Kathy got up too, watching the woman, all her apprehension suddenly restored, her stupidity hung out again like a wreath on a gravestone.

'Who is it?'

Ma scowled and waved her hand. She looked just the same as she had done in the house, with curlers in her hair and the giant cotton sack of the nightgown draped around her.

'Early breakfast indeed, Storer,' Ma grumbled into the receiver. 'You've a nerve. D'you know what time it is?'

Ma waved again, changing hands on the phone. 'All right then, Storer. Ay, I suppose we'll be there. Give's ten minutes though.'

She slammed down the phone and heaved her heavy legs over the edge of the bed. She looked tired. Kathy said, 'Are you . . . all right?'

'I'm fine,' Ma said. 'I'm just annoyed. Come on, lass, up y'get. Storer wants us in the lounge. Ach, what a trockle this all is.'

In spite of her protests Ma readied herself swiftly enough and within a quarter of an hour was leading Kathy into the lounge. It was all dark now save for one band of light over a corner table. Storer sat there alone, with a pot of coffee and three cups on the cloth before him. The young night porter passed them as they entered, yawning, but happy with the heavy tip which Storer had given him. It was cold in the room with the heating turned down. Ma drew her cardigan more closely around her.

When they seated themselves, Storer poured coffee. He looked exhausted too, Kathy thought, and wondered if all his sleeping was done in snatches in armchairs. She saw him as a man in almost constant motion, coming to rest at times like this when some necessity dictated it. She fretted about what the necessity could be. Perhaps the hotel was not safe. Perhaps they would have to move on again, take another long ride in the Porsche, carrying her into another phase of the dream.

Storer said, 'I won't keep you long.'

'Come on, out with it,' Ma said.

Storer sipped his coffee and added more sugar. He did not look at Ma. 'I . . . I just wanted to make sure you were okay.'

'Y'what?' said Ma loudly. 'Y'got me up in the middle of the night, just t'make sure . . .'

Kathy found herself saying, 'We're all right, Mr Storer.'

It obviously came as a surprise to Storer that she called him by his name. It never struck him that his identity was known to her. It had just happened. Ma had called him Storer several times.

Storer mumbled, 'Good, good', and buried his face in his coffee. Then he looked up again, 'Can you drive?'

'Yes.'

'Do you hold a licence?'

'Yes.'

'How about you, Ma?'

'Ay, I can drive, but I haven't for years,' Ma retorted. 'Don't tell me y'fancy a wee spin round the sights of London.'

'It's snowing still,' Storer said. He peered off beyond Kathy's head for an instant, off into the dark corner of the room. Then he was staring at Kathy. He said, 'A man will come to the table in a couple of minutes – he's on his way now – he'll look at you and he may ask you a few easy little questions . . .'

'Is he a policeman?' the girl said.

'No,' said Storer smiling. 'He's not a policeman. Just answer him, that's all. Just answer his questions and then you can both go back to bed.'

As he finished speaking a well-dressed middle-aged man appeared at Kathy's elbow. It seemed to her that he had materialised straight out of the floor like a pantomime demon. He did not appear particularly demonic however, just sad, spaniel-eyed, chalk-faced, and stared at her as if she was Helen of Troy reincarnated. Storer did not introduce him, and the man paid no attention at all to Ma MacAusland. Kathy saw his tongue licking his lips.

'What's . . . your name?' he asked.

'Kathy,' she said. 'Kathy Arden.'

'Arden?'

'Yes.'

'Where do you live?'

'I don't . . . I was born in Manchester, if that's what you mean.'

'Tell me.'

'Tell you what?'

'Tell me about yourself.'

'There's nothing to . . .' She turned to Storer. 'What is all this?'

'It's all right,' Storer said. 'We're not white slavers. Just answer his questions.'

'I lived with my mother until she died. Last year, she died last year,' said the girl.

'Are you an only child?' said the small man.

'No,' said Kathy. 'I have a sister, but I haven't seen her in years.'

'And what is your sister's name?'

'Rena.'

'Do you know where she is?'

'No.'

The man stopped speaking. He turned his head towards Storer who was still drinking coffee, drinking it hurriedly now as if it was a rare tonic which would revitalise him and renew the strength which he had lost.

'All right, Storer.'

Storer put down the cup and got to his feet. 'You can take her back to your room now, Ma.'

'Thank you very much,' said Ma sarcastically. 'Who the hell is he?'

'I'll see you tomorrow,' said Storer. 'I mean later today.'

'What d'we do all day?' Ma asked.

Storer shrugged. 'Sleep.'

'Huh!'

Then he was gone after the man, walking fast through the vast palatial spaces of the lounge, his feet making no sound at all on the carpeting. Under the arch, framed against the light of the lobby, Kathy saw the men pause and the older peer up into the younger's face as if pleading for an explanation. She thought she saw Storer's lips moving and then the man nod emphatically. Storer took him by the elbow and ushered him out of sight.

Bewildered, she rounded on Ma. 'Who was he? Why am I important?'

Ma shook her head. 'I'd tell you if I knew, lass, but I'm as much in the dark as you are.'

'He asked about my sister,' Kathy said. 'Does my being here have anything to do with her?'

'I don't know.'

Kathy thought for a moment, then said, 'I'd like to meet up with Rena again. I really would.'

Ma got to her feet. 'Maybe you will,' she said. She yawned, stretching one heavy arm as if reaching for the dull glitter of the chandelier. 'Maybe you will – someday.'

10

Saturday was a busy day for Storer. After he got the word of approval for his plan and delivered Rushton back to the Stag's Palace, he had himself some breakfast and a lot more coffee in a workers' café. Around seven-thirty he returned to the Gresham and packed two bags. Without calling on Rena, he paid his bill and promised the proprietress that if ever he was in London again he would certainly stay at her hotel. He was back in the Porsche by eight and drove out through the struggling dawn into Kent.

He drove fairly slowly, observing as he went. As he came out on to the Orpington by-pass the sun came up under the clouds. Wreaths of mist drifted off the fields and parklands, the thin covering of November snow seemed to make no difference. Crows paraded like a convention of crippled widows in the bottoms, and the copses stood up naked and delicate against the molten edge of the iron-plate sky. Most of the traffic on the roads was against him, but he held the Porsche at a steady fifty. He turned off east along the course of the Darent towards Crumlington. The developments lay to the London side of the village, and behind hedges and wicker trellises he caught an occasional glimpse of lights in big square kitchen windows. He whipped through the high street of Crumlington out into the monied area which shaped up back from the roadway, aloof behind stands of elms and parkland all white and hazy in the first pink flush of the sun. There was a tiny church, and a little graveyard with some antique stones pushing hauntingly through the snow. When he passed the entrance to Rushton's house he checked the time on his watch. He knew he could shave a good half hour off the trip if he had to, given roads free from ice and fog. A mile down the road he swung into a lay-by, turned the Porsche and drove back to London.

He turned up in the Stag's Palace after making the usual phone-call. Everything seemed normal downstairs, but when Burchill admitted him to the suite Storer at once sensed the urgent and anxious preparations that were going on. Rushton had back a lot of his old steeliness and Storer hoped that the old man had given Burchill no hint that he knew of his treachery. Within ten minutes Burchill was in the midst of outlining the plan to Storer. Storer played it up as if he had heard none of it before, adding his dollar's-worth of comment, helping to tighten the scheme just as if it was all going to happen as scheduled and he knew exactly which side of the fence he was on.

So far they had been lucky and had attracted no attention from the law. Though this operation was on a grand scale Burchill surmised that no word of it would leak out in time for the fuzz to take an interest in what was going on at Grassleigh Common. There were no banks or private art collections, no railway tracks near by to focus the Yard's attention on the place. Storer ate lunch in the Palace, but left shortly after two, allocating to Burchill the reconnaissance of the Common and the setting up of accurate interception points on the route. No sign passed between him and Rushton, no wink or nod or clue of any sort. He promised to be back at the Palace by seven next morning.

He left the Porsche where it was, collecting the two bags from the back before he locked it. He walked to Leicester Square and caught the Underground to Waterloo. He booked into a hotel there and went directly to his room on the third floor. First he unpacked the money from one bag and sent the bell-boy out for a gift box and wrapping paper. While he waited for the boy's return, he counted out a thousand for himself, added it to what he had left of Rushton's original five hundred and spread it about the pockets of his suit. When the bell-boy returned with the materials, Storer neatly boxed and wrapped the remaining nine thousand and addressed it to Mrs A. MacAusland at her hotel. Then he wrote a letter, sealed it and Scotch-taped the envelope to the outside of the parcel. He put the parcel beneath the bed. Next he cleaned his gun and set it out with the knife in readiness. Finally he showered and dressed again and went down to eat an early dinner.

By seven, with a couple of vodkas inside him, he was in bed. Beside him on the table the alarm clock kept a soundless record of the minutes and held its spring ready to waken him at six o'clock. When that time came it would be Sunday and the last act of the double deal would be under way. By this time tomorrow he would be either rich or dead. In spite of the clanking in the heating pipes and the Saturday night roar of traffic, he had no difficulty in sleeping and, being Storer, did not dream.

Part Four

1

It was ten to seven when he reached the Stag's Palace. He left his gear in the hotel, carrying with him only his weapons and the money. The sheepskin coat covered it all but it was loose enough for him to be able to reach the gun in a hurry. He had tipped the bell-boy extravagantly and left the parcel with him, giving him precise instructions that it was to be delivered at ten o'clock to the written address.

Snow had come down overnight, but only in a couple of light showers which freshened up the city again and covered the slush that the traffic had made on the roads. Storer was nervous, with an ache in his stomach, and did not touch the breakfast which Rushton had laid out on hot-plates in the suite. No one ate much. In the hour before departure time only Burchill seemed cool. He put out a last series of telephone calls, checking with Mills and Marquand, working openly from the phone on the desk in the lounge. Presumably his plan was all set out and needed no expansion at this late hour.

At half-past eight the diamonds were delivered by two of Marquand's men. The Jaguar in which they arrived was protected fore and aft by two identical vehicles with two armed men in each. The diamonds were in a brown paper parcel, long and flat and heavy. Rushton did not unwrap it, and Storer wondered if the stones inside were real. The banknotes were real enough for he had watched Burchill make up the parcel. At nine exactly he and Burchill carried the parcels down to the Mercedes at the kerb at the back entrance of the club. Rushton accompanied them and there were others too, discreetly placed about the entrances. The convoy of Jags had gone on ahead to check the agreed route for ambush possibilities and to bolster the forces around Grassleigh. Representatives of Mills and Marquand, and one of Rushton's more trusted men, would follow the Mercedes at a discreet distance in a Land-Rover, brought along in case cross-country pursuit was necessary. It would follow at a pre-arranged speed a steady quarter of a mile behind.

Burchill got behind the wheel but as Storer made to enter Rushton gripped him by the arm and pulled him back a pace.

'Storer,' Rushton murmured. 'You'd better behave.'

'I want my money,' said Storer. 'That's all.'

'Hm,' Rushton said. 'But you'd really better behave. You see, I have the girl and the woman, and I'm sure you wouldn't want anything to happen to them.'

'Where are they?'

'Quite safe,' Rushton said. 'And they'll remain quite safe, provided you get me that briefcase. Do I make myself clear?'

'Yeah,' Storer said.

'Go on then,' Rushton said. 'And be careful.'

'Yeah,' Storer said again.

He got into the car and Burchill handed him the parcels which he put on his knee. Rushton slammed the door for him and the Mercedes started off.

'What was all that about?' Burchill asked. 'Something wrong?'

'No,' Storer said. 'He just told me to be careful.'

'As if you wouldn't,' Burchill said.

Storer waited until they turned the first corner out of sight of the Stag's Palace, then he put his hand into his pocket and took out the gun. He held it low on his lap, shielded by the parcels.

'All right, Burchill,' he said. 'Do exactly as I say, or I'll kill you.'

Burchill glanced at the snub nose of the weapon and grinned. 'You didn't waste much time, did you, Storer?'

'Did you want me to wait for you to draw first?'

'With my hands on the wheel too,' Burchill said. 'No.'

Storer said, 'Step on it, Burchill.'

Obediently Burchill put his foot down on the gas and the big car smoothly picked up speed.

'Next left.'

'I suppose you're after the money, Storer,' Burchill said. 'All for yourself.'

'Nope,' Storer said. 'I'm after the briefcase. *Left I said.*'

'Ooooops,' said Burchill and turned the car sharply.

'And right.'

'And right,' repeated Burchill, obeying instantly. 'You wouldn't be trying to lose our supporters, would you?'

'Left now,' Storer said. 'Not so fast.'

'As you say,' Burchill said. He slowed slightly and took the Mercedes easily into the corner, drove on a hundred yards and stopped at traffic lights. Storer reached forward and broke the connection on the radio, watching Burchill all the while. Burchill drummed his fingers lightly on the steering wheel.

'Where are we going, Storer?' he asked. 'I assume it's not Grassleigh Common?'

'We'll cross at Vauxhall Bridge,' said Storer. 'I'll direct you from there.'

'You wouldn't really put a bullet in me?' Burchill said. 'Rushton wouldn't like it.'

'Rushton would love it,' Storer said. 'But your friends Mills and Marquand might be a bit piqued.'

'Oh!' said Burchill. He frowned a little.

'And no doubt Rena would cry her eyes out.'

'Rena,' said Burchill. 'Did she put you up to this?'

'Bloody-well you know she didn't,' Storer said. He sat square on to the driver with his back against the nearside door, the gun steady in his lap. 'You had me marked for the sucker in this game, didn't you, Burchill? I was marked as the one who tried to buck the syndicate and flog off with the quarter million. I suppose the idea was to flush out Rushton, Lenihan and Browning all in one go, using the rigged accounts.'

'Rigged accounts?' said Burchill. 'I don't know what you're talking about.'

'In the briefcase,' Storer said. 'Those accounts aren't genuine; they're doped to set the law on the three, while you and Mills and Marquand stand clear till the dust dies down. Then you step in and the pot's all yours – a three way split instead of a five.'

'Balls.'

'You should have kept Rena out of it.'

'It . . . it was her idea,' Burchill confessed. 'She suggested it in the first place.'

Storer tapped the parcel on his lap. 'Is the ice genuine?'

'Marquand's not crazy,' Burchill said.

'What does that mean?'

'It's real,' Burchill said. He was silent for a moment; then he said, 'Look, Storer, why don't you just walk off with them, and the money too – a quarter of a million; it's a lot of loot for a simple stick-up.'

'And what would you do then, Burchill?'

'Tell them you planned it,' Burchill said. 'That you were in with Rena all along. As you were, come to think of it.'

'I didn't know the whole story then,' Storer said.

'You don't owe Rushton a thing,' Burchill said. 'Go on, step out of the car and vanish, man. You've got the loot, what more do you want?'

'I want the briefcase,' Storer said.

'Not very wise,' Burchill said. 'You can't hit them for any more blackmail money. They won't pay. I doubt if Rushton will survive this knock. Once Marquand puts the pressure on him he's finished. At least we'll get that out of it for our money. All right, Storer, I'll admit it. We want Rushton out of the syndicate. Now will you help us?'

'The briefcase,' Storer said.

'It's in my flat,' Burchill said. 'Back in Belgr . . .'

'Don't lie, Burchill. I know where it is.'

'Did Rena tell you?'

'God,' said Storer. 'Do you *want* her to turn on you? Okay, Burchill, I'll give you a cross to bear. Rena has a couple of little tricks up her sleeve, but ratting to me isn't one of them. I'm supposed to kill her sister and pass the body off as hers. In that way she hopes to take the heat off.'

'Crazy,' Burchill said. 'It sounds exactly like her. I knew about it, though the big two didn't. Rena's not important to them now. That was your part in it, Storer, to put down the sister and fake it up.'

'Yeah.'

'But you didn't,' said Burchill. 'Why not? You don't have a moral conscience?'

'It wasn't feasible,' said Storer. 'Anyway I had the smell of rat in my nostrils by that time.'

'I think,' said Burchill, 'we all put a little too much on your plate.'

'You and your boss and Rena,' said Storer. 'I was working for all of you simultaneously, even if I didn't know it.'

'That you were,' said Burchill. 'Who are you working for now?'

'Myself.'

'Then get out of the car with the diamonds and . . .'

'Keep driving,' said Storer.

'Where the hell are we going?' said Burchill. 'Have you a boat lined up?'

'I told you,' Storer said. 'We're going to pick up the briefcase from the place you hid it.'

'Where?' said Burchill smugly. 'You're only bluffing.'

'In Crumlington,' Storer said. 'In Rushton's house.'

'Really!' said Burchill. 'You've blown out, Storer. What the hell would it be doing there?'

'The last place he'd think of looking would be in the safe,' said Storer. 'It was pretty obvious you'd hide it back there right after you doctored the car to make it look like robbery. Rena in her Ventora was well away by that time.'

'Clever,' said Burchill. 'Wrong, but clever.'

'We'll see,' Storer said. 'We'll see.'

'What, now?'

'That's where we're going,' Storer said. 'Right now.'

'All right, Storer,' Burchill said. All the levity had

gone out of him. 'I'll take you there, but I just hope you're not in for a shock.'

'Drive faster,' Storer said. 'We may not have too much time.'

2

'I don't know who you think y'are,' Ma MacAusland said, 'but I wish you'd stop wavin' that gun at us.'

Hulme looked sharply up at her as if she had spoken in a foreign tongue. He was a large man and fitted the car coat so full that the seams of the quilting were stretched almost to bursting. He was closer to the woman's age than to the girl's and he did not like the job he had to do. Micky was downstairs in the kitchen brewing up cups of Nescafé for them all. It had been thoughtful of Rushton to hand him a carrier full of groceries, for the house was chilly and the bloody great ice-box in the kitchen empty as a tomb.

Hulme had seen Rena several times; he wasn't sure that it wasn't the boss's wife who was tucked up in bed in front of him, sleeping like a baby. The boss had told him it wasn't, but even so Hulme wasn't sure. Maybe he would have a chance to talk it over with Micky and see what Micky thought. Micky was younger than he was and brighter too: Hulme would be the first to admit that in the brains department he wasn't a top man. The woman's attitude worried him more than the girl's. The girl was all sort of meek, not particularly frightened – which added to his conviction that she was Mrs Rushton – but the woman had been growling with anger since he had turned the gun on her in the car outside the hotel. He gathered that she had expected Storer, which was why she came so meekly with Rushton. By the time she realised she'd been duped it was too late and he had the gun on her. He didn't much like turning a gun on a woman, especially in a London street, but the boss was watching so he had to behave and do what he'd been told to do.

Sunshine flooded the windows. Through the nice lace curtains it cast a shaft which struck the bevel of the mirror of the dressing-table. Some bloody room, Hulme thought, like a bloody palace. The whole place was very pukkha-pukkha. He wouldn't have a place like this and go on living in the city, not if he could help it. Own grounds, servants' quarters, space in the garage for four limousines and nothing for miles around but trees and fields. Not that he liked the country much, but he certainly liked the house. God, as Micky said, he could get his own three rooms in the kitchen and still have space for a snooker table. The sun dazzled him a little and he shifted the soft armchair a couple of feet so that his view of the woman would not be impaired. If only she would get into bed and all, sleep like the young one, then maybe he could lock them in and go for the leak he'd been needing since they arrived. What the bleedin' hell was Micky up to there?

'What's the idea, son?' the woman said. 'Are y'goin' t'starve us t'death?'

'In a minute,' Hulme said. 'He'll be here in a minute.'

She occupied the chair in the corner as if it was a throne, sitting back in it with her legs square and her arms on the side of it just like a queen. She wasn't scared of him or the gun, she was just mad, seething away quietly like a vat of home-brewed beer.

'What's your name?'

'Hulme,' he said, almost without thinking.

She grinned evilly. 'Hulme?' she said. 'I'll bet your old man was wee Peter Hulme from Bayswater – the burglar.'

'Yer,' said Hulme in surprise. 'How did yer know that?'

'Did eight in the Scrubs on his last term and died about five minutes after they let'm out.'

'Yer. Did yer know him?'

'Ay,' said Ma. 'I knew him.'

'Who're you then?'

'Inspector Hall of Scotland Yard,' she said in a bass voice. 'Heavily disguised, of course.' She laughed as Hulme stared, half believing her.

'Getterway!'

'I wisht I could.'

'Well, yer can't.'

'If it wasn't for that gun I could *take* you,' she said, leaning forward.

Hulme involuntarily pulled himself back and cocked his wrist to bring the gun up on her. 'Eh?'

'In single combat,' the woman said through her teeth, 'y'wouldn't stand a chance against me. Women's Services Karate Champion five years runnin'.'

'You were?'

'Ay, I was,' said Ma. 'Like t'try it on?'

'Sit down,' he shouted as she pressed her hands on her thighs and made as if to rise.

She sat down again, stared hard at him for a minute, then said, 'Where's my breakfast?'

'Belt up, for God's sake,' said Hulme. 'Yer worse than the wife.'

'Ha!' said the woman. 'I'll bet y'never pointed a gun't her.'

'Why can't yer go t'bed like the young 'un?'

'Where are we?'

'Never mind.'

'Who's your boss?'

'Never mind.'

'What's he want with us?'

'Never bloody mind.'

He got up, because he was afraid of her, and held the gun out the way they did in all the movies he'd seen, elbow bent at the hip and forearm straight. He noticed that the snub sight was wavering a little, and tightened his grip.

'Plug me, kid,' the woman said. 'Go on an' plug me.'

'Hell!' Hulme said. He sat down once more but did not stop watching her for a second.

Outside the snow on the ground made the light blue and the blueness was in the mirror. He could see the girl's face in the mirror and her eyes were closed. He did not even trust her now, suspecting some sort of plot between the two of them to catch him out. She was pretty, the girl was, with her blonde hair spilled out on the pillow and her lips parted. Some girls looked better when they were asleep; the bitches did, for sleep softened the harshness of the lines of their faces, but others looked horrible. His wife looked horrible when she was asleep; she looked even worse when she was awake.

'It better be porridge, son,' the woman said. 'I'll complain to the management if it's not porridge.'

He said nothing. He had decided that she was baiting him to get him to do something foolish and he did not entirely disbelieve her story about being a lady karate champion. Maybe she just wanted to get him close enough to nobble. In this silence he heard what might have been the crunch of tyres on the gravel of the path. He was relieved that the chore would soon be over. Tempted to go to the window he restrained himself, listening hard but hearing no other sound.

The door opened and Micky entered carrying a tray with breakfast on it. A wisp of fragrant blue steam came from the glass lip of the coffee pot. Hulme sniffed it appreciatively. Micky put the tray on the dressing-table, pushing aside hair brushes and combs. Micky was squat and over-muscled but had a bland, blond cherubic face with large silky blue eyes. He didn't look too bright, but he was. Micky would go a long way with Rushton and the syndicate. Hulme was glad to see him. The woman got to her feet and came hurriedly towards the tray, but Micky rounded on her rapidly.

'Get back,' he snapped.

She stopped. 'I'm starvin'.'

'You'll get it,' Micky said. He had real command, had Micky. 'You'll get it when I say so, so get back to yer corner, missus.'

She was mad again, buzzing mad, but apparently karate champ or not she was unwilling to tussle with Micky. She returned to the armchair in the corner. Micky walked to the bedside and scrutinised the girl.

'Leave'r,' the woman said. There was a different tone in her voice now, protective. Micky was shrewd enough to recognise it as a danger signal. He had been told not to harm them, and he would not disobey his brief. Besides, it was better if the girl went on sleeping.

Hulme said, 'Can I go for a leak?'

'Yer,' Micky replied.

Hulme had only just reached the door, tucking the gun into his jacket pocket, when the sound of the car on the gravel became unmistakable. Micky was at the curtain in a flash, holding it up with his wrist and peering out from behind it. Hulme stood in the open doorway with the gun out again, covering the woman.

'Who is it?' he whispered.

'Burchill,' Micky said. 'Hey wait, there's . . .'

'What's up?'

'Somebody with him,' said Micky, bewildered. 'With a gun in his back.'

'Eh?'

'They're coming in,' said Micky. 'Jesus, that's queer.'

'Maybe we should go down there an' . . .' Hulme began.

Micky cut him short. 'Listen,' he said. 'Just keep cool, Hulme, okay. No rush. I don't think the geezer with the gun knows we're here.'

'You sure, Micky?'

'No, I'm not sure,' said Micky. 'Listen, you stay here. Keep them shut up – her especially. If she peeps then club her one: okay?'

'Yer.'

Hulme hurried to the window. 'What about our car?'

'It's garaged,' Micky replied. 'They haven't spotted it.'

Through a corner of the curtain Hulme caught a glimpse of Burchill. He was walking across the path towards the front door, his hands in the air and an expression on his face like that of a man on his way to a firing squad. Behind him was a tall figure in a sheepskin coat.

'That's Storer!' Hulme exclaimed in dismay.

He wheeled round, but Micky had gone.

The woman was hovering over the breakfast tray with a quarter of toast in her fist. She wiped butter from her mouth.

'Storer?' she said.

'Don't tell me you know him too?'

She shook her head and poured herself coffee. 'Och, no,' she said. 'I just like the sound of the name.'

She grinned and casually buttered another slice of toast. Storer was the last thing he had bargained for. Hulme was afraid now, really afraid. He just prayed to God that Storer was on their side, though by the look of the gun in his hand he was against them all the way.

3

The rhododendrons against which the Mercedes was parked had gathered white buds of snow in the hollow of their leaves, and glistened in the sunlight. Once he had Burchill out of the car and the car locked, with the parcels still safe inside, Storer had time to inspect the front of the house. It had a neglected look about it, deserted. The windows were all curtained and there was no signal of smoke from any of the red brick chimney stacks; they were probably imitation anyhow. The front door was barred across by two huge oak panels. Off to Storer's right was a croquet lawn fringed by evergreen bushes trimmed to phallic shapes and capped with snow. Storer told Burchill to head for the rear of the house. Burchill veered right around the gable towards a conservatory built against the wall. The door of the conservatory was not locked and they went inside. Even with the cold outside the morning sun had warmed the air under the glass. Another door led straight from the conservatory into what appeared to be a study. This door had glass panels and it was locked.

'Break it,' said Storer.

'I'm no burglar,' Burchill complained.

Storer swung his right foot and kicked Burchill on the base of the spine. Burchill cried out in pain and catapulted forward.

'You bastard, Storer.'

'Now break it,' Storer said. 'There's a spade in the corner.'

Burchill lifted the spade from the corner of the conservatory and Storer stepped back a cautious couple of paces as Burchill drew back the blade. He may not have been a burglar but he was strong enough to force the door with one blow.

'Put the spade down and go in.'

Burchill did so and Storer followed him into the study.

The room smelled of the rows of unread books on the wall shelves and the heavy drapes and the leather chairs and sofa. There was an antique desk over by the window.

'Is it here?' Storer asked.

'What?'

'The place where you hid the case?'

'I keep telling you, I didn't . . .'

Storer kicked him again, making sure that his shoe struck the tenderest area it could reach. Burchill snarled and turned on him, showing his teeth like a cornered dog-fox, but the gun held him off.

'Where is it?'

'In the lounge.'

'You'd better not be stalling,' Storer warned.

They passed carefully through the house. In the hallway Storer stopped again, his back protected by the wall, listening. A staircase ran up to his right and through the props of the balustrade he could see the bedroom doors on the first floor landing, all closed. In the lounge just ahead of them sunlight streaming against the floral curtains printed patterns on the paper. Down another corridor Storer saw the gleam of a tiled kitchen. He did not know what made him uneasy. Perhaps it was the smell in the air, an odd smell, like the faint aroma of coffee.

'Go on, Burchill.'

They eased into the lounge.

All the furniture was draped with dust-sheets, except the cocktail bar. On the walls were gilt-framed landscapes any one of which was large enough to cover the mouth of a safe.

'Where?' Storer asked.

'Oh, don't you know?' said Burchill acidly. 'I'm surprised; I thought you knew everything.'

'Cut the chat,' said Storer. 'Where's the bloody safe?'

A large sheet of opaque plastic draped the hearth, pinned to the mantelshelf with heavy brass ornaments. Storer put the sofa between him and Burchill then gripped a corner of the plastic and swept it away. The ornaments crashed to the stone of the empty fireplace. Burchill winced at the sound and whipped a glance over his shoulder. Storer knew then that he had him for sure. Burchill was finally losing his cool. Now that the time had come for a show-down Roy's nerve would not hold out for a bluff. Storer did not know whether he would have shot Burchill or not: possibly he would have put a bullet through his shoulder or his thigh just to get him going. Whey-faced now, Burchill bit his lip: then he shrugged, his arms rising high into the air as if reaching for an invisible ladder.

'Over here, Storer.'

Storer nodded. Burchill crossed to the cocktail cabinet, lifted the gate and went behind it.

'It's below,' Burchill said. 'Done out to look like an ice-box.'

'Clever idea,' said Storer. 'Now open it.'

'I don't have the combin . . .'

'Open it.'

Storer leaned on the counter and kept the gun on Burchill who got painfully down on his knees before the plain metal door inset into the solid wall back of the bar. Using the chrome button-handle Burchill tugged the door open. Behind it was the stout green panel of a safe and the dial of a combination lock. Burchill brushed his fingertips down his lapel and looked up at Storer. Storer nodded and Burchill set to work on the dial. After a few moments the safe door clicked open and revealed its dark depths. Storer took a peanut from a bowl on the bar and shoved it in his mouth. It was stale and wooden and salty but he nibbled it with his teeth.

'Take the case out slowly,' he said. 'And put it on the bar.'

The briefcase was of black blocked leather, with a nickel lock. Burchill slid it to the bar top and came up after it.

'Hands high,' said Storer. He pulled the case towards him, watching Burchill still, fully aware that any instance of relaxation would cost him dearly. The brief-case was locked and when Storer asked Burchill for the key the man only shook his head. Storer dropped the case to the floor and stamped on it until it flew open.

The accounts were heavily detailed, but a cursory glance was sufficient to tell Storer how valuable they would be to the authorities. Names and quantities, prices and shipment numbers, a cipher of illegal trading all around the world. He noticed the words like Bremen and Amsterdam, Oslo and Geneva. He re-folded the sheets, stuck them back in the case and tucked it under his left arm.

'Satisfied?' Burchill asked.

'Sure,' said Storer. He motioned with the gun and Burchill came out from behind the bar.

'What now,' said Burchill. 'I suppose you bump me and run for it.'

Storer shook his head. 'Sit down.'

Puzzled, Burchill lowered himself to the nearest armchair, the dust-sheet billowing around him. Storer hoisted his haunch on to the back of the couch.

'What the hell are you waiting for?' said Burchill. Sweating profusely, his nostrils flared, he showed every sign of being very scared. The sight was not pleasant and gave Storer no satisfaction.

'We're waiting for Rena,' Storer said. 'What time is she due?'

'Rena?' said Burchill. 'Rena? I don't get it, Storer. What do you want with Rena? Are you going to kill her too?'

'I'm not going to kill anybody,' said Storer. 'Unless I'm forced into it. Rena *will* be here, Burchill. She'll come for the case, and she'll come soon. Grassleigh isn't that far away. I suppose the idea was for you to put me out then Rena would vanish for a while until Rushton, Browning and Lenihan were well and truly scuppered, then you'd come back and take up your rightful place at Mills's right hand. These accounts would be despatched to the Yard, or the Tax authorities and the diamonds would find their way back into the organisation by a devious route. The fifty thousand cash was intended to keep her in style, out of harm's way, for a while. You'd blame me, a dead man, for being in it with her and *you'd* come out without a blemish. Am I right?'

Burchill showed his teeth again, but this time it was intended to be a grin. 'Not quite, Storer,' he said. '*They* wanted Rena dead. Mills did. I knew about the sister.'

'When's she due?'

'What time is it?'

'Ten after ten.'

'Any minute,' said Burchill. 'They'll be following her now, of course, since we got lost.'

'Is she using the Ventora you got from Maurice Fortune yesterday?'

'You *have* been busy,' said Burchill. 'I always thought it was a mistake to bring you in on it.'

'But you needed a convincing fall guy,' said Storer.

Burchill was very quiet now; the grimace had eased into a smile. He looked . . . confident. Storer frowned. Burchill leaned back in the chair, his hands clearly visible even among the puffy folds of the sheet.

Burchill said, 'I suppose you'll keep the money?'

'Yeah,' said Storer.

'Rushton's money?'

'Yeah, but . . .'

Suddenly Storer became aware that Burchill was looking past him, bright and glittering eyes fixed on the doorway, a smile fixed on his mouth. Storer rolled, pivoting, and dipped into the shrouded couch. He felt a savage stab of pain in his left shoulder an instant before he heard the noise of the gun. By that time he had fired twice, his face pulled back and his right arm extended over the ghostly balloon of linen cloth.

Micky grunted and his jaw sagged in surprise. His second shot came out after he had begun to fall and the bullet went high, shattering the glass of a mirror over the hearth. Storer did not stop to allow the pain to consume him. He lunged round and met Burchill's rush with the blade of his left hand. It smacked under the nose and he felt Burchill's head snap away from him and heard the crunch of breaking bone. Screaming like a girl, Burchill reared back and staggered round in the space between the furniture. Storer brought the gun butt down across his skull, then he went down in a heap on the rug and the only movement from him was the gush of blood from his nostrils. Storer whirled again to the door but no one was there, just Micky's body huddled over the drooping automatic, his brow resting on the post, like a duty guard who has fallen asleep.

Storer knew there were others in the house: instinct told him so, but how many or who or where they were was more than he could say. The wound in his shoulder was bleeding badly but the bullet had gouged through flesh only and he had, as yet, no serious loss of mobility in the arm. He was glad of that. He went over to the corpse by the door and pulled it away from the opening. He recognised the man as one of Rushton's, but could not tell whether he had shifted his allegiance to Burchill or not. Anyway, he was dead. From the corpse's trouser pocket Storer took a set of car keys. The fob was a shamrock of shiny green metal rubbed smooth by use. He put the keys into his own pocket, collected the briefcase and, leaving Burchill unconscious on the floor, shifted out of the lounge.

He was on edge now, every nerve in him honed up to a razor-sharp fineness. He hugged the briefcase in the crook of his left elbow, as a shield across his heart. It wouldn't do much good, but the gesture comforted him a little. He sidled around the wall of the hallway, keeping watch both upstairs and down into the kitchen. One of the upstairs doors was ajar and even as he watched it opened and a face peered cautiously round it. Storer knew him: Hulme. Storer froze against the wall, his body screened by a small granddaughter clock. He watched Hulme nose out of the bedroom, cocking his head this way and that to see through the spars of the balustrade. Hulme had a gun in his fist and was keyed-up enough to fire at anything that moved. Even at the distance Storer could see the globules of sweat on the man's brow. What he saw next startled him. He had to fight to hold breath tight in his throat. Framed in the bedroom doorway, directly behind Hulme, was Ma MacAusland. In her hand she carried the steaming glass coffee pot, holding it out from her gingerly. Then Storer understood. At the same instant Hulme saw him. Storer dropped to his knee.

The first bullet destroyed the clock-face, piercing the convex glass dead centre and going on into the mechanism with a jangle of wires and springs. The handsome little clock rocked on its pedestal and toppled away as Storer flung himself full length across the wood-block floor. He was looking at the long score in the polished wood which Hulme's second bullet made and already turning with the gun, frightened to squeeze the trigger in case he hit the woman.

'*You, Hulme,*' Ma shouted.

Caught off guard, Hulme wheeled half round and took the boiling glass coffee pot full in the face. It splintered on contact, showering him with scalding liquid and slivers of glass. He reeled and tottered across the landing clutching his blinded eyes. The automatic was still in his fist but he did not fire. Storer rolled over, rose and hit the staircase running. He took the steps three at a time, stooped low. Looking up he saw Hulme towering over him, waltzing like a trained bear across the top step of the landing. Storer sunk his head into Hulme's gut, heard the man roaring as he lifted him and threw him, in one gigantic bull-like tossing motion, over his shoulders. Hulme spread-eagled in the air then landed ten or twelve steps down, like a high diver who has mistimed his twist and strikes flat. Storer heard something crack, ribs maybe, and Hulme bunched and expanded and bounced down the rest of the flight to fetch up wide-armed far out in the hall. Before Hulme stopped twitching, Storer was in the bedroom and had the door locked.

4

The girl Kathy was seated on the side of the bed with her head held to one side and her fingers clapped over her ears. Storer put his hand on her shoulder and she flinched as if he had struck her.

'It's all right,' he said.

She took her hands away and stared at him, her eyes round with fear. Then she gave a great shuddering sigh which seemed to take all the terror out of her as if it had lurked like a poisonous gas in her lungs.

'You're hurt,' she said.

'Yeah,' said Storer. He grinned at her. He had no reason to grin but it came naturally to him in spite of the pain radiating from his shoulder. He winked at the girl and turned to Ma. 'Just two?'

'Ay, just the two of them. Are they dead?'

'One is,' said Storer.

'Let m'see that shoulder,' said Ma.

'In the bathroom,' Kathy said, 'there's stuff in the bathroom. Is it safe . . . ?'

'You're sure,' said Storer, allowing Ma to help him off with the coat, 'you're sure there was only two of them?'

'Certain,' said Ma.

'All right,' Storer told Kathy. 'Bring me something to dress this wound.'

The girl left the room and turned right on the landing. She did not look down into the hall, as if she realised that there was something below which it would be better not to see. Storer grunted as the sleeve of the jacket came away. Blood flowed freely and in the centre of the wet red patch the shape of the bullet hole stood out like a badge. Ma found a pair of manicure scissors on the dressing table and cut away the shirt sleeve around the seam. Storer was relieved to see that the bullet had apparently only furrowed the surface flesh.

'You'll live,' Ma said. 'Were they after Kathy?'

'They'd have killed her,' Storer said.

'I fell for it,' Ma said. She tutted between her teeth and lifting a corner of the bedsheet pressed it tightly against Storer's shoulder. 'I thought the message was from yourself, son. It was from the joker y'brought to the hotel.'

'I know,' Storer said.

'Did y'know we were here?' said Ma. She gave a curt self-conscious chuckle, with little mirth in it. 'Was it a rescue?'

'Was it hell,' said Storer. 'I didn't know where you were.'

Ma nodded and watched the web of blood appear on the linen.

Storer said, 'Let the girl think what she likes.'

'My God, he wants t'be a hero,' Ma said.

'Will you?'

'Ay,' said Ma with a sour mouth. 'Ay, ay. It's no skin off my nose.'

A moment later Kathy returned bearing a glass of water, towels and a first aid kit still sealed in its card-board box. She opened the box and set out antiseptic and bandages on the bed where Ma could reach them. She knelt by Storer's knee, looking up at him. Her skin was as pale as milk and her eyes large, but otherwise she seemed quite composed.

'The man in the hall,' she whispered, 'is he dead?'

'I don't know,' said Storer.

'Should I . . . should I do down?'

'Better not, lass,' Ma said. 'Not at the minute.'

Storer was sweating with the pain in the shoulder but the tension had not gone out of him yet. He was listening hard for the sound of the car. After Ma had bathed the wound and set about dressing it, he drank what was left of the water in the glass, then he said, 'Listen, I want you two to get out of here.'

'What about you?' the girl asked.

'Quiet,' Ma told her. 'Quiet an' listen.'

Storer took the keys from his pocket and held them up to her on his palm. 'Kathy,' he said, 'take these. You and Ma go down to the garage where you'll find a car. Get in and wait in the car with the garage doors closed. You may hear sounds – all right, shooting – or you may not. Stay there until I give you a sign. If you hear shots or the sounds of cars in the driveway, wait fifteen minutes *after* the last noise, then open the garage doors and drive out of here.'

'What about . . .?' the girl began.

'Never mind about me,' said Storer. 'It's important that you get away clear.'

'*Why* am I so important?'

Storer shook his head ruefully. 'With luck,' he said softly, 'you may never know.'

'I don't . . .'

'Shush,' said Ma again.

'Ma, I'll give you something, accounts sheets, from this briefcase, and two parcels. The square parcel belongs to us.'

'Money?' said Ma.

'Yeah.'

'How much?'

'Enough to see both of you on your way,' said Storer. He looked hard at Kathy. 'Will you go with her?'

'I don't want your money,' the girl said firmly.

'I earned it,' Storer said.

'By killing?'

'It's not stolen,' said Storer, 'and where it came from

it won't be missed. It's mine now, and it'll be yours. For Christ sake, take it.'

'What else?' Ma said.

Storer glanced at his watch, wiping blood from the glass. He began to talk rapidly, dogmatically. Neither of the women interrupted him. 'Take the road south-west out of here and drive back to London via Croydon. Do you think you can manage that?'

Kathy nodded.

'Go straight to your hotel, the one I left you in, and pick up another parcel there. It's at the desk in your name. It's yours too. Wait an hour for me in the lounge. One hour, but not a minute longer. If I don't show in that time take a cab to the Stag's Palace, it's a club off New Compton Street in Soho. The cabbie will know it. Have him park round the corner, Ma. Leave Kathy in the cab with the two square parcels. The car you take from here you'll leave at the hotel: dump it, ditch it. You, Ma, you take the flat parcel and the accounts and go to the club. Ask specifically for Rushton ...'

'Is he the ...?'

'Yeah, that's him. Ask for Rushton and tell the doorman Storer sent you. He'll let you in. Give Rushton the accounts and the flat parcel. You must see him in person. If he asks about the other parcels tell him you don't know anything about them. If he asks about me, or . . . a man called Burchill, or if he questions you, tell him nothing.'

'I don't know anythin' t'tell him,' said Ma.

'Right,' said Storer.

'Won't he try to hold me there?' asked Ma.

'I doubt it,' Storer replied. 'He'll have what he wants, and he won't know enough to make it worth the risk. Nope, he'll let you go. Get down to the cab again, go to Euston and catch the next train to Glasgow.'

'Glasgow?' said Ma.

'It's as good as any place,' said Storer. 'You'll be going home.'

'M'home's in Watford.'

'Maybe,' said Storer, 'you want to die there.'

'Ay,' said Ma. 'It would be nice t'see Glasgow again, come to think of it.'

'Today is Sunday,' Storer said. 'Book into a hotel somewhere out of Glasgow centre, and lie low. Next Sunday take a trip to Loch Lomond and lunch in the Duck Bay Hotel. If I can, I'll join you there.'

'An' if you don't?' said Ma.

'Then you're free.'

For a moment there was silence. Kathy looked questioningly at the woman. Storer got up and slipped into his jacket again. The pain was going out of the wound now but the wad of dressing hampered his movements a little. He rolled the shoulder to make it more mobile.

'What about me?' Kathy said. 'Why should I do all this for you?'

'Not for me,' Storer said. 'For yourself.'

He went to the window, gently lifted the curtain and looked out at the silent grounds. Around the bottom of the shrubs the snow was beginning to melt off, fretting and thinning to expose the sodden lawn beneath. A small avalanche of slush poured from the house roof and hissed to the path beneath. The sun, close to its winter zenith, shone full on Storer's face. He turned. 'Do you both understand?'

'Ay,' Ma said.

Kathy nodded.

'All right,' said Storer. 'Let's go.'

'Storer,' Kathy said. 'Why can't you come with us now?'

Storer opened the door and went out into the upper hallway. In the silence a dying tick from the shattered grand-daughter clock which had spilled its works across the parquet, was as loud as a rifle shot.

'Storer?' the girl said, just behind him. 'Why can't you?'

'I have an appointment,' Storer said. He did not tell her that they would not make it with him along. Ma understood and the girl would go with her: that was all that mattered. 'Yeah,' he said, almost to himself, 'a very important appointment.'

He took the gun out of his pocket and moved cautiously downstairs.

5

When it was all done and the two women were in the front seat of the Jaguar, Storer returned to the house. Ma had the money and the diamonds and a folder full of the faked accounts. He had almost completed his contract to Rushton, but it was not over yet.

His shoulder was hurting again, but he did not think of it, nor did he think of Kathy's troubled eyes and the quizzical quality in her voice when she asked him, 'Will I see you again?'

'Sure,' he'd told her. 'Sure, you'll see me again. You've got my money, haven't you? You'll see me again.' Then he'd walked away and pulled down the door of the garage on them. It was all fixed. Ma would do as he'd told her and the girl – well, he thought the girl would hold out too. In the confusion and in the fear she would cling to Ma. There was affection between them and a kind of dependence. He didn't have time to work it out how it came about or what was to be the outcome of it. They were drifting, drifting along when he came and gave them direction; now he had shoved them off and he was alone again.

Hulme was dead. He dragged the body into the lounge and laid it out behind the door. He gathered up the wreckage of the clock and threw it into the lounge too. Burchill was still out cold, the blood-stopped nostrils snorting as if the anger in him defied even unconsciousness. Storer left him where he was, went out again and closed the door on the mess in the lounge. With him he carried the shell of the empty briefcase, Band-Aid taped over the broken lock to hold it shut. All he needed was Rena. He planned on using Rena as a decoy. If he left with her and the briefcase it would look like another cross. At this stage, Mills would not stand for it. All he had to do was get the pursuit after him and far enough away from Crumlington to let Kathy and Ma make a clean break. Mills and Marquand had no way of knowing they were here anyway: perhaps did not even know of their existence. His thinking was good enough. They would follow him, follow the man with the brief-case, like hounds on the scent of a hare.

He had been at his post in the entrance to the conservatory only a few minutes when he heard the sound of the car. It carried clear in the cold air from a long way off and he had to contain his agitation until the roar of it grew and finally it squealed to a stop in the yard. He counted up to five then stepped round the gable with the gun in his hand and the briefcase under his arm. Rena was caught between the Ventora and the entrance to the house. She gaped at him in astonishment. He grinned and came on towards her. Other sounds were coming up through the silence, the faint throb of a helicopter and the whine of cars on the road below the house, like the noise of insects in the air.

'Hello, Rena,' he said.

'Storer!'

'I was supposed to be dead by this time, wasn't I?'

'Where's Roy?'

'Inside.'

'Is he dead?'

'Nope.'

'You've got the briefcase, Storer, and the diamonds, why don't you get out of here before they . . .'

'No,' said Storer. 'We're going together, you and I.'

'I won't, Storer. I *can't* go with you.'

'They'll try to put me down, won't they?'

'Yes.'

'And if you're in the car too then it'll be your hard luck.'

'Yes.'

'Maybe I should take your sister instead,' Storer said.

'Kathy?' said Rena. 'Where is she?'

'Safe,' said Storer. 'Get in the car.'

'Why are you doing this, Storer? What can you hope to get out of it now?'

'Fifty thousand and my neck,' Storer replied. 'Perhaps. Now get in the bloody car.'

She hesitated, then turned on her heel and climbed back behind the driving wheel of the Ventora. Storer did not move from the exposed spot in the middle of the gravel yard.

'Don't try anything, Rena,' he called out to her. 'I'll shoot you if you do.'

Her face was expressionless and bloodless, so that the spots of rouge on her cheeks stood out like dabs of paint on the china skin of a doll. 'There are too many of them, Storer,' she said. 'You'll never make it.'

'Maybe not,' Storer said.

He stood waiting, listening to the sounds come closer and closer until at last he saw the shadow of a helicopter circle the grass of the lawn. He did not take his eyes off Rena, but the shadow was obvious, like the leathery wings of a huge prehistoric predator. It came round again, unable to circle too low over the house top. This time Storer looked up. The sun glittered on the windows and whirled into a static silver spray on the blades. He thought he could discern two men inside; then it dipped towards him and a first round of gunfire eratically peppered the rhododendrons. He held out the briefcase and ran, sliding into the Ventora just as Rena slammed it into gear.

'No,' he shouted. 'Not yet.'

The helicopter was dropping rapidly, hanging above the clearing in the centre of the croquet lawn. The slipstream of the rotor blades summoned up the last loose particles of snow in a rainbow storm. Even before the runners touched, two men leapt into the fine veil of snow dust.

'*Now.*'

The Ventora bounded forward. He did not have to tell her what to do. He had committed her and bound her fate in with his; to stay alive she had to act as he wanted her to, even without instruction, using only the instincts with which she had concocted the whole deal and set up the deadly reaction which put them both on the line now. She was already fisting the wheel. The tyres ate into the barrows of unmelted snow where the gravel verge joined the grass, and the car slewed broadside to the lawn. At that precise moment the men emerged from the low blizzard and Storer had a clear shot at them. He dropped one with the first bullet, but the bucking of the car disturbed his aim and when the second figure went down he knew it was not in death. He could not be certain but he thought it was Marquand.

'*Again*, Rena.'

And again the Ventora knitted a circle, spraying stones and slush in a wave which, so tight was the turn, hissed and rattled against the panels. She pulled the car out, scraped by the shrubs, the off-side wheels over the grass lip, and slowed it almost to a standstill.

The pilot leaned from the cabin of the chopper: he had a rifle. He sighted and fired and the spang of metal on metal came from somewhere back of them. Storer shot and the pilot floated up, the rifle spinning out of his grip like a cheer-leader's baton, and then he pitched forward and dropped to the ground. Marquand – it was Marquand – sprinted for the cover of the nearest bush, diving the last few feet like a panther, his body outlined against the snow. Storer put two at him but did not appear to hit: then the Ventora was feeding fast out of the top of the turn. Storer yelled, '*Drive. Drive*', and the house went past them and the nose dipped into the avenue between the wall of shrubs. Storer swung round in the seat just in time to glimpse Marquand at the lawn's edge, down on one knee, the pistol raised. The shots were muffled, faded fast and came nowhere near the Ventora. With a last kick, the back end snapped out of the yard and trees blocked off his view of the lawn, the house and the garage. He noted with relief that the door of the garage was still closed.

Rena was chattering at him, cursing him, calling him all the lunatics and madmen and bloody fools she could think of, but her eyes were on the avenue ahead and he knew she was only letting the fear out of her in this way. He attended to the gun, looking up only when she yelped at him, looking up to see the Jaguar spurt out of the corner at them. It was on them instantly but the driver, indistinct behind the sheened windscreen, had apparently spotted them first and mounted the car up on to the soft shoulder. For a moment it seemed that the heavy machine would cant and topple with its own weight but it held, tilted above them, as Rena shoved the Ventora to the inside of the curve. It crashed along the bushes and cleared the tail of the Jag by inches.

'Oh, God, Storer,' Rena was screaming. 'What am I doing here? Why don't I *stop*?'

'You can't.'

'*Yes, I can, yes,*' she said. 'I can explain . . .'

'They'd pump you full of bullets before you could open your mouth,' said Storer.

The Vauxhall careered to the foot of the drive where Rena regained enough composure to slow down before emerging into the roadway. The second Jaguar, caught in the act of sweeping into the drive, swerved wildly to avoid them. It snouted into the gatepost with a jarring crunch which split the white-painted post and tossed the upper part across the bonnet. Fleetingly

Storer saw the horror in the face of the man at the controls and the passenger's arm fended up as the wood shivered against the glass.

'Move it, Rena,' Storer shouted.

The Ventora pulled wide into the road, straightened out and, as Rena gave it gas, took off like an arrow. Sun-dazzled, the reflection from the window hid her face and not until the rising bank cast its shadow over them did Storer notice that she was weeping. He would have preferred to take the wheel and thought longingly of the thoroughbred Porsche lying up there in London; he really had need of it now. Anyhow, it was impossible to stop and change places, and besides he did not trust his wounded shoulder to stand up to the strain of fast driving. Only by depending on the woman's nerve and skill could he hope to escape. Both Jags would be in pursuit by now but so sharply contoured was the country road that he could not tell just how close they were. The Jags would surely outstrip them on a straight, or at least come within effective range. With a sag in the gut he remembered the submachine gun; it would really make mincemeat of them if it was brought into play. The Ventora settled at maximum speed, Rena up on the seat's edge scanning the way ahead for black ice. The tyres ripped harmlessly through the flimsy crusts of the verge puddles but a stretch of hard water-ice would finish them for sure. They passed through a hamlet and ran on into a tunnel of trees, climbing slightly. Storer turned round and through the back window saw the Jags weaving nose to tail less than a half mile behind.

A gradual curve rose to the summit of a little hill below which pasture and woodland spread before them like an ornate quilt worked with silver medallions of snow. The foremost Jag crept stealthily up to narrow the gap to fifty yards. It came looming out of every corner now showing the dented teeth of its radiator like a sinister leer. At a cross-roads, the Ventora crossed the bow of a stationary tractor. A farm-hand sat up high on the seat. His head swivelled phlegmatically to watch the Ventora and then the Jaguars go rocketing by. He was still staring after the traffic when a burst of gun-fire perforated the settling silence; then, dodging and jockeying for position, all three cars were gone. The farm-hand shook his head and wondered vaguely what would happen to those loony speedsters when they reached the hairpin and the bridge at the end of the ribbon of road.

The first spray from the sub-machine gun flayed the rear off-side window and showered particles of glass in on Storer. Automatically Rena tucked down her head and, as her control frayed, the Ventora sawed about. The second burst played on the roof like peas on a drumskin. Even through the padding Storer could see the long gouges dug out convex on the inner side. It was only a matter of time until one of those rounds chopped the tyres to ribbons.

'Lay-by ahead,' he roared. 'Turn in and brake.'

She nodded frantically, shoved the wheel hard and slammed down on the brake pedal. The Ventora skidded and snaked into the crescent clearing by the roadside and stopped dead. The Jaguar plummeted past it.

'Get down.'

Rena obediently ducked and, resting his forearm on her shoulders, Storer pumped bullets through the open window of the cabin as the big car flashed by him. They were in motion again before he had time to gauge the effect; he felt sure he had hit something though. The lagging Jaguar spat at them, but after the ferocity of the sub-machine gun's volleys single shots seemed as harmless as flies. Rena had the Ventora out of the lay-by before Storer could open his mouth, and ranked it behind the vanishing hindquarters of the car in front. She too knew the desperate gamble he had made, sandwiching them between the two Jags. For a minute Storer began to think they had lost, then abruptly the car ahead slewed and shuddered and climbed, sleek and vertical, up the banking and, still full of power and grace, vaulted the hedgerow clean as a bird, all in the air, and nose-dived straight into the trees. Flame burst out, great orange sheets of it, fringed with black smoke like ostrich feathers round an exotic silk gown. A solitary figure, a fire-ball with legs, trotted out of the wreckage and raised a pair of burning arms up to heaven like a victim of self-immolation drawing the attention of the gods to his rash act. Storer saw no more as the Ventora hurled him away towards the hairpin and the stoop-shouldered bridge.

Rena negotiated the double bend skilfully without dropping too much speed. The remaining Jaguar had to come down too far and they gained a few more precious yards. They were still firing from the passenger window: Storer could see the shooter's head and arm, but it gave him no anxiety for it came to him that his luck was holding good and that the odds had shortened enough to offer him the ghost of a chance of winning this deadly game. He watched with a certain admiration as Rena poured the Ventora up the humped back of the bridge. Then the back window disintegrated and Rena's hair was wet with blood. Her head slumped on the wheel. The back of her skull had holes in it and she was dead.

It all seemed to happen slowly, so slowly that Storer felt like a man imprisoned in a dentist's chair who is impatient for the pain to begin so that it might be over sooner. Reflex made him grab at the kicking wheel and push her legs away from the pedals but the force shot her forward and she sagged over and he could do nothing. The car butted the tail-post of the bridge and spun broadside. It went through the fencing side-on and still spinning, the violent motion whipping Storer out of his trance. The tyres burrowed through the snow into firm winter mud as the car slithered into a region of tall reeds and grasses. The marsh sucked at it and checked its mad flight just long enough for Storer to throw open the door. Then the Ventora lost contact with the earth, lay over and wallowed down through a scum of ice. It turtled instantly and sank into the deep black waters of the main channel, dragging Storer with it.

6

Far downstream Storer broke surface. He had allowed the current to carry him, scissoring his legs to keep the weight of sheepskin from dragging him to the bottom. The resistance of the ice told him that he was approaching the shallows but he held himself still under it. All the air in his lungs was used up and the bitter cold gripped him mercilessly like a massive iron fist, squeezing him towards insensibility. Mud squirmed under his fingers. He floated on to his shoulder, pushed forward another yard, lifted his nose and mouth out of the water and gulped at the air like the first amphibian testing a new and alien element. Lifting himself higher yet he saw that he was partly sheltered by a cove of reeds and that the bridge was surprisingly distant. He dragged himself on to the mud bank. A man was framed above the keystone of the bridge, the sun and the strike of it on the roof of the Jaguar fashioning an aura round him. Two other men were plodding down the opposite bank inspecting the gashes that the Ventora's tyres had made. They stopped at the point where it had entered the river and talked together. Perhaps they were debating how to recover the briefcase, or whether or not Storer had drowned.

Rena was dead, but Storer was too sick to feel any sorrow for her. The man on the bridge shouted an order. Sprawled half out of the water Storer shielded his eyes and peered through the reeds. Had they spotted him already? To his relief he saw the searchers on the bank turn away. He had lost his gun somewhere in the river and needed a gun, and the car if he could get to it. Possession of a gun and the Jaguar were his only hopes. They were going to search for him and his trail would not be difficult to find. Reinforcements were certainly on their way by now. Marquand would have seen to that. He had recognised the figure on the bridge. He would kill Marquand if he could, Storer decided.

He gathered his strength and wriggled on to solid ground. The grasses rustled by his elbows and wreaths of snow among the roots sank crisply beneath his knee. Exhaustion overwhelmed him: he lay back and contemplated the blue sky like an angler on a hot summer's afternoon. He thought how sad it would be if that second helicopter appeared overhead and desecrated the pristine emptiness of the sky. The silence was utter, save for the faint subtle gurgles of water filling the holes he had made in the mud and the lonely cawing of a rook in the distant trees. Finally he rolled on to his belly and propped himself up to see what was happening. The two on the river bank were in consultation with Marquand on the bridge, calling up to him. Marquand: a cold hatred steeled Storer and drove him on. He started off, crawling through the grass veering a little to the right, knees and elbows working in earth-hugging mole-like action which carried him at fair speed towards the road. The activity warmed him and after a few minutes he stopped shivering and his lungs no longer seemed full of frozen acid. A bird, a duck of some sort, batted up out of the reeds just ahead of him, squawking a loud warning to its kin. Storer lay as still as a log for several seconds: he did not dare look up to see the effect of the bird's tell-tale flight. He could hear no sound near him and after a while went on again. Finally he judged himself to be well clear of the line of the bridge and stuck his head up. The two men were on his side of the river-bank now, guns in their hands, searching half-heartedly among the reeds. Marquand was leaning over the bridge contemplating the river. Storer was too far off yet to risk a sprint either for the roadway or the shelter of the trees on his right. His strength was gone and he had no reserves left to draw upon. Dropping to his belly, he cut right, choosing the trees as his best escape route.

Shortly, the reeds thinned, gave way to tussocky grass and finally to an exposed plane of snow-dappled pasture. He could go no further under cover and was still thirty yards short of shelter. He fished the knife from its sheath in his jacket and held it in his right hand. Not far off was a low knoll, and not too far beyond it a cluster of alders which, though winter stripped, would provide him with some scant protection. It was all he had: it would have to be enough. Against the sky a plume of oily smoke rose straight from the tree tops under which the burned wreckage of the Jaguar would lie, perhaps already surrounded by police and farmers. Someone was bound to have noticed the smoke. It would not be long before outsiders arrived here too. He blinked at the alders again, then in sudden decision scrambled to his feet and ran. He threw himself over the knoll, tumbled down the slope on the other side, got up and sprinted for the alder brake. Shouting echoed in the air, and a bullet hummed over his head. They were on to him again.

He drove himself hard, weaving crouched through the trunks towards a wall ahead, not knowing what lay behind it. He kept his head tucked into his chest. Just as he flung himself against the dry-stone, metal chipped on a boulder close by his ear and sang off. He climbed the wall, rolled across the top and fell into the snow, with the spit of two more bullets on the edge above. With the mist gone from the graveyard the old stones had a benign beauty in the midst of the snow. Against the trees the squat tower of the little church stood out like a toy. Storer stumbled through the monuments and over the shrouded graves and reached the corner of the church before the first of his pursuers appeared over the wall.

The entrance to the church was dungeon-like, down a flight of worn stone steps below ground level. A wrought-iron grill in the oaken door allowed Storer to look inside. He saw a sparse sunlit interior, a tiny altar, a lectern and a handful of plain pews. The black-iron bolts on the door were strongly fastened by a padlock which he could not force, but he remained there pressed against the woodwork, peering into the church, craving the peaceful illusion of security which it gave him, the inviolable haven of a place in which death itself would be clean and spartan and tinted bright. He tore himself away from the grill, backed up the steps, hauled himself along the wall to the rear of the building. There was no scrap of shelter there either, only an old barrow with its rusty wheel in the air and a few warped planks. The acknowledgement of his hopeless situation gave him a measure of serenity. He permitted himself to dream vaguely of how pleasant it might be to bring Kathy here and wander round, looking at the gravestones and the church. It must be beautiful in summer. Abruptly he wrenched the stupid yearning from his mind.

Resting his shoulders against the stone, he stared at the long naked blade of the knife in his fist. He was hardly aware of fatigue, or the pain in his shoulder, or the sodden clammy weight of the coat. Momentarily the inside of his skull was as unencumbered as the empty church, devoid of enmity or ache, devoid even of the cunning which had always been part of him. Now stirring through his thoughts came the final vain notion that he might yet escape. He crept forward and lifted one of the planks. The wood was weathered to a fine dove-grey, the grain smooth against his flesh. He picked out a knot with the knife-blade, unplugging a hole large enough to take two fingers; with the plank held across his body like a battle shield, he sank back against the wall and strained his ears for informative sounds. Ironic that he, Storer, who had lived most of his life alone, should connive to take someone into death with him. Whoever came around that corner would be his companion. He hoped it would be Marquand. Instinct told him they were close. He shook his right arm gently to ease the stiff muscles and took proper hold on the knife. An instant later they were on him.

As soon as the figure was fully clear of the corner he leapt out and drove the knife blade into the man's gut, struck twice in rapid succession, feeling the blade slide in and out and in again. The victim's face was close to his own, framed by the angle of the timber and the plane of the gable, the expression shifting from shock into agony and finally congealing into a passive smile which mocked the violence of the knife. The automatic slipped from the dead fingers. With the plank Storer took the full weight of the slumped body and fended it off, stooping in the same motion to grab the gun. As his hand closed on the butt a bullet seared his neck, a sudden scald like the lash of a bull-whip. Swinging round, he took the next shot deep in his left shoulder. He dropped to his belly and lifted the automatic. Marquand, squatting, extended his arm with the pistol, barrel and sight and fist on the grip all foreshortened. Flat on his fallen plank, Storer fired twice with perfect aim at Marquand's heart and tilted his third shot to the brow. Marquand went back as if he had been kicked, his hands travelling up but not quite reaching the star of blood between his eyes.

Storer did not have to search for the third man. Two bullets ripping into his thigh told him where to find him. Even as bone shattered and blood started hot and quick down his chilled flesh, Storer fired the automatic for the last time. The man toppled over the fence, a bubbling sound in his throat like a drunk vomiting. The gun slipped from his grasp and slithered a few yards down the ice-slope by the fence post.

Slowly Storer turned his cheek against the plank and squinted along the ground. Marquand's carcase was twisted like a grotesque briar root, a bright red dart on the snow where the impact of the bullet had flung his head back. It was clean though: not like the death of the Negro, Storer thought, not like the sweating flesh and the welter of blood spewed out in the confines of a shabby room. Not at all like that thing, that horror, but clean, somehow pure. Still clinging to the plank like a boy on a surf-board skating down the crest of a long and powerful wave, he inched his face round again. He saw the figure on the fence drape the wire, doing it ponderously as if it was a difficult acrobatic trick which he had not quite mastered. One foot hooked on the uppermost strand and he hung there, the overcoat spread out around him like fleecy wings, rich and gaudy and regal.

Storer stared down the length of his own body and saw that his thigh too was stained crimson. The warmth of blood gathering in the hollow of his groin soothed him. With his brow against the solid, grey-bleached plank and the dazzle of snow in his eyes he waited. A rook croaked raucously in the trees and the sky was icy blue. Patiently he waited, knowing it would not take long.

7

'Sit down.'

'I'll stand.'

Rushton nodded and lowered his head to scrutinise the sheets which were spread on the desk before him. Ma folded her arms and scowled at the bald spot on Rushton's scalp as if it held a window through which she could see the machinations of his brain. Finally Rushton sighed and took off his glasses. He rubbed his eyes, then squinted up at the woman, inclining his head away slightly as if her size intimidated him.

'Where is he?' Rushton said. 'Where's Storer?'

'I told you already,' Ma snapped. 'I don't know. He just gave me those . . .'

'Yer, yer,' said Rushton. 'But it's not enough. I got to know what's happening.'

'Well, I'm not the one t'tell you.'

'You must know what happened to my men,' said Rushton, pleadingly. 'Hulme and Micky: at least you must know about them.'

'They went away with Storer,' Ma lied. 'I never saw them after that.'

'Oh, Gawd!'

Ma leaned forward and placed her hand flat on the sheets between Rushton's elbows. 'You've got what y'wanted,' she said. 'Is that not enough for you? He kept his part of the bargain.'

'Where's the girl . . . what's 'er name . . . Kathy Arden?'

'Outside in a taxi,' said Ma. 'Where I'll be too in a minute.' She peered into Rushton's face, her brows so deeply furrowed that the skin stood out like two flint arrow-heads. 'I've done what Storer told m'to do, an' that's the end of it.'

She swung away towards the door.

'Wait,' Rushton cried. 'Wait.'

He struggled to his feet and came after her. Ma stopped and wheeled on him and in his anxiety he bumped into her. She snatched at his arm to stop him falling. He looked scared, sweat on his temples and his jowls as white as unleavened dough. 'It's my house,' he stammered. 'I g-g-g-got to know what's happened there.'

Ma drew herself up and her bosom rose full and threatening like that of a fighting hen. 'Storer won't take it kindly if you hold m'here.'

'Damn Storer,' said Rushton, adding hastily, 'All right, all *right*.'

She gave him a little shove and he reeled back. She pulled open the door. The guard looked round hurriedly, but Ma shoved him too. Before he could touch her in retaliation, however, Rushton ran out of the room. The man gave way to his boss, and Ma was descending the stairs, not slowly but not hurriedly either. Rushton leaned on the railing.

'Where are you going now?' he called.

She did not deign to glance back, but her voice lifted clearly up the stairwell. 'None of your bloody business.'

Behind Rushton both telephones in the suite simultaneously began to ring. Rushton tried to ignore them, to tear himself away from their infernally insistent sounds; he knew only too well that the messages they carried would not be good news. With a final neurotic gesture of despair and capitulation he stalked back into the lounge and slammed the door with his heel.

Ma MacAusland went on down to street level. No one tried to stop her or paid her the slightest heed and she emerged from the back exit into the lane and turned left into the main street. She had gone along it only a few paces towards the corner round which the cab was parked, when two cars pulled up outside the Stag's Palace. Neither had whirling lights nor wailing horns but Ma recognised them at once. She paused curiously and for a moment watched the men in overcoats and soft hats climb out of the vehicles. There were five of them and she could tell by their pace and eagerness that they considered their business urgent. Wanting nothing to do with the law, she quickened her step and took herself round the corner out of harm's way. The taxi was waiting, and Kathy was still inside. With a little inaudible groan of relief Ma hoisted herself into it and sank thankfully down on the seat.

The driver folded his newspaper. 'Where to now, lady?'

'Euston Station.'

On her knee Kathy held the two sealed parcels steady with her arms as the cab started up and swung into Tottenham Court Road. She glanced at the big woman thoughtfully but said nothing. Ma too was silent for a while. The sunny Sunday pavements uncoiled alongside. Overhead the sky was deepening to lavender with approaching dusk, and the only snow still visible clung to the ledges and eaves of office blocks and cinemas. Ma put her hand on the girl's arm.

'You don't have to come with me, y'know,' she said.

'He told me to.'

‘Ay,’ said the woman, ‘but I’ve the feelin’ it won’t matter now.’

‘I’ll come all the same,’ the girl said.

Ma plucked the string of the parcel. ‘If you’re worried about your share . . .’

‘It’s not that at all,’ Kathy retorted. ‘You owe me nothing.’

‘I’m thinkin’ maybe I do,’ said Ma.

‘I’m coming to Glasgow with you,’ said Kathy firmly. ‘And next Sunday . . .’

Ma shook her head and her flat mouth kinked at the corners with the sly trace of a smile. ‘Next Sunday we’ll keep our appointment with Storer?’ she said. ‘Ach, lass, you could spend the rest of your young life waitin’ for the likes of Storer.’

‘Do you think he’s . . . dead?’

The woman shrugged. ‘Could be.’

‘But if he does come . . .’ Kathy began.

‘You want to be there?’

‘Yes.’

‘He’s not worth it.’

‘Perhaps not,’ said Kathy, ‘but I’ve nowhere else to go.’

‘Nowhere?’

‘Nowhere,’ the girl replied flatly.

‘Ay,’ said Ma softly, ‘then maybe we’d just better do what Storer told us.’

The cab drew to a halt. The driver got out and opened the door on the pavement side, but neither of the women moved.

‘What if he doesn’t come?’ asked the woman.

The girl thought for a moment, then shook out her bright blonde hair as if to dismiss the question. ‘We’ll see,’ she said.

'This 'ere's Euston,' the cabby said. 'You gettin' out?'

'Yes,' the girl said and, carrying the parcels, stepped down to the pavement. The big woman followed her. They paid the fare and then went off, walking slowly and together, towards the north-bound trains.